SPAWN POINT ZERO

DEFENDERS OF THE OVERWORLD

BOOK 3

Nancy Osa

Origins matter . . .

Sky Pony Press

New York

Copyright © 2015 by Hollan Publishing, Inc.

First Edition

This is a work of fiction. Names, characters, places, and incidents are from the author's imagination and are used fictitiously.

Sky Pony Press books may be purchased in bulk at special discounts for sales promotion, corporate gifts, fund-raising, or educational purposes. Special editions can also be created to specifications. For details, contact the Special Sales Department, Sky Pony Press, 307 West 36th Street, 11th Floor, New York, NY 10018 or info@skyhorsepublishing.com.

Sky Pony® is a registered trademark of Skyhorse Publishing, Inc.®, a Delaware corporation.

Minecraft® is a registered trademark of Notch Development AB.
The Minecraft game is copyright © Mojang AB.

Visit our website at www.skyponypress.com.

10 9 8 7 6 5 4 3 2 1

Library of Congress Control Number: 2015945383

Cover illustration by Stephanie Hazel Evans
Cover design by Brian Peterson

Print ISBN: 978-1-5107-0321-6
Ebook ISBN: 978-1-63450-0322-3

Printed in Canada

For my friend Lil

SPAWN POINT ZERO

The cavalry commander glanced at the soldier by his side. Frida's smudged olive-green face showed internal and external scars from the misadventure they had just survived. She was tough, but she was also complex.

In fact, it had been the wiry scout's sixth sense for truth, not her battle skill, that had impressed Roberto from the beginning. His respect for her had blossomed into a greater esteem that he'd only lately acknowledged. They had become partners by accident. Who could have guessed when they'd met—two individuals from vastly different planes—that they would hold the fate of the Overworld in their hands? Whatever they did next would either resurrect a representative government, and the freedom it promised, or throw the reins of power to the dark forces.

Would they be forced to go it alone? Their four friends had been delayed, perhaps permanently. A player could sustain only so much damage before respawning became impossible. But the slim chance that rebirth could occur had pushed the other members of Battalion Zero to make the ultimate sacrifice. Rob and Frida had been encouraged to run and not look back, in the hopes of saving the union, dealing out justice, and maybe . . . just maybe . . . reuniting at their base camp.

Together, the six cavalry mates had successfully defended biome borders and seen a capital city rise from the hills. Now the time had arrived for Rob to define *his own boundaries. Knowing where he'd come from and where he wanted to go wasn't enough. He needed to decide whether to devote himself to this place and these people—or to keep searching for a way home.*

Again he looked at Frida. His mind and heart ached to remain with her; his urge to leave this world was fading like an old pair of jeans. Did it really matter where they were if they couldn't be together in the moment? If the captain had learned anything from recent events, it was that time might be more important than space in this game. Maybe the future depended on how he came to terms with his past.

CHAPTER 1

ROBERTO SCRIBBLED A LINE, CROSSED OUT A FEW words, and sat back with a sigh. This writing stuff was harder than roping, riding, and herding cattle put together. One thing that writing and riding herd had in common, though, he noticed, was the need for stick-to-it-iveness. Slacking off wouldn't get cattle to market or this advertisement written and posted for all to see.

"And nobody's gonna spur me on to finish the job," the cowboy-turned-cavalry-commander muttered. He returned his attention to the marked-up page.

Just then, a hairy black spider crawled into view. It scuttled toward him. Trying to concentrate, Rob drew his iron sword and let the arachnid impale itself on the blade. Instinctively, he reached for the string that dropped and the creature's eye, which bounced on the ground a few times, before it could roll away. *Distractions, distractions,* he thought, idly wrapping one end of the string around the eye and the other around his hand, and batting the eyeball with his palm.

He realized what he was doing and threw the toy away. *Think!* he commanded himself.

After a bit more work, he'd completed a satisfactory draft. It read:

PIONEARS WANTED

New United Biomes of the Overworld capitle city under construction seeks villagers and players looking to relocate. No investment nessissary. City of Beta offers:

- **start-up economy**
- **family-friendly atmisfere**
- **protection from mobs and greifers**

Approved immigrints recieve free shelter, month's supply of food, and access to jobs. Beautiful extreme hills location. Apply Beta City Hall.

"What's that you've got there, sir?" asked Stormie. She'd left her TNT crafting to see what the captain was doing. The fit, dark-skinned young woman appeared capable of providing strong offense or defense, with or without explosives.

Rob frowned, trying not to gawk at her black crop top and shorts. A cavalry commander's attitude toward his troops had to be strictly neutral. "It's an ad for the new city, Private. But I'm not sure about my spelling. . . ."

She took the paper from him and read it to herself, lips moving. "Just a few mistakes, Captain. Sounds good, though. I'd apply if I weren't already here." Her contagious grin spread to Rob.

"Thanks." He took in the camp the battalion was setting up, and the larger construction project under-way up the hill. These settlements were dwarfed by a mountainous slope that rose in stair-steps to the sky behind them.

"Just think of the possibilities," Stormie said to the captain. "At this moment, it's the perfect city."

Rob wished he could share her enthusiasm. There was no telling what type of element his advertisement would attract. He ran a tan hand wearily through his shock of black hair. "City's only as perfect as the people in it."

"Or the ones behind it," Stormie insisted.

In that case, Rob thought wryly, *we'd better add another coat of paint.*

Rob couldn't help worrying about his troopers' dedication . . . not to mention his own. The cavalry had spent months battling griefers and hostile mobs before the city had even taken shape. Now the six players itched to return to their chosen lifestyles: Stormie to rambling the globe; Frida to solitary jungle survival; Turner to exchanging muscle for gems; Jools to selling strategies; and Kim to raising and training horses on her beloved sunflower plains. Rob's greatest desire lay not in this generated world, but in the larger place from which he'd come, not so long before—a peaceful Western range that he hoped to find again. He'd been flying back there from vacation when he found himself tumbling through space, into a whole new ballgame. Given that his spawn point was a moving airplane above an ocean, going home would be . . . problematic, to say the least.

Down in the valley, where Rob now stood in his customary chaps, vest, and cowboy boots, springtime flowers had begun to bloom. Their vigor and promise seemed to herald the new city. "This is it, then," he said. "We're nearly open for business." Pride and panic washed over him. This latest effort would bring either salvation or doom to the Overworld—and which one was anybody's guess.

"It's a brave, new world, Captain," Stormie said, taking in the landscape.

At their feet spread a lush vale of flower-specked, turquoise grasses, crisscrossed by sparkling blue streams that tumbled from snow-fed waterfalls. Above them rose the extreme hills—precipitous heights touching the clouds—dividing the world hemispheres and nearly isolating them. From down here, the intricate rock sculptures formed a gallery of cliffs, canyons, caverns, and cantilevers. From up there—as Rob well knew—the unobstructed view created a topographical map of every biome as far as the eye could see.

The already picturesque spot was being transformed into a site worthy of its purpose—the first capital city built in the Overworld since the destruction of Alpha in the long-ago war. The unified government had operated piecemeal from each of the dozens of world biomes for years. During that time, dark forces had attempted to wrest the land from its residents— until Battalion Zero had ridden in to stop them.

Now that the opposing griefer alliance had been subdued, a central seat of power had become practicable. Rob and his cavalry were among a handful of hopefuls who debated the idea. In the end, the Overworld's defenders had come together to boost the project . . . once their arguments had all been exhausted.

*

MONTHS EARLIER

"Only zombie pigmen would want to move to a place like that!" grumbled Turner. Although he was the battalion's sergeant at arms, the deeply tanned, tattooed mercenary disliked the prospect of enforced order. "Far as I'm concerned," he said, "town full of lawmen and lawmakers is barely a step up from the Nether."

"Which, you'll recall, is complete chaos," Jools said, drumming his pale, slender fingers on the long table around which they sat, surrounded by their battalion mates and advisors. Jools's previous work as a detail consultant allowed him to see the big picture in most scenarios. As cavalry quartermaster, he meticulously kept track of resources and offered a practical voice of reason. He put in his valuable two cents now: "What we need is a happy medium."

"Typical, coming from you," Frida, the company vanguard, threw in. "Just because you don't like to take sides, doesn't mean everybody in the Overworld holds the middle ground."

Jools hiked up the sleeves of his tweed jacket and leaned across the table. "While you'd prefer to go it alone, right? I'm surprised you're even considering defending a capital city. If I'm not mistaken, you're the original renegade, hailing from a long line of bitter loners."

Frida's olive-green face darkened a shade. "Look who's talking. How long did it take you to pick up a sword and fight with us?" A loner by birth, the survivalist had still given her all to the battalion's cause—and with less prodding than the quartermaster had needed.

Frida's friends, Stormie and Kim, glared at Jools, daring the avowed separatist to continue his attack.

Captain Rob put up a hand. "Now, now, let's take it easy. This is a focus group, not a reality show. Judge? Colonel? Where were we on the agenda?"

The top members of Battalion Zero—Rob, Turner, Jools, Frida, Stormie, and Kim—had met in the conference room with their advisors, Judge Tome and Colonel M, to hammer out a strategy for building a new Overworld capital. First they'd see if it was doable. Then they'd decide whether to commit to the mission.

Colonel M cleared his virtual throat. He had lost track of the proceedings, and would have shrugged his shoulders if he had any. The old veteran had escaped the definitive First War battle with only his head, which had grown to twenty times its size upon respawning. It now sported a wild thicket of silver hair.

Judge Tome, a bespectacled justice of the peace, thumbed through the sheaf of papers before him, searching for the group's written agenda. Although retired from official service, the judge maintained a distinguished presence, with his clipped, whitish-gray hair and neatly manicured fingernails. He adjusted his black cloak and then located the page he wanted. "Here we go. Let's see. We've covered 1-A, location; 1-B, community buildings and residences; and 1-C, food and water needs. We should be on 1-D, transportation and defense."

Rob perked up. Horses and horse soldiers, he could handle.

Judge Tome continued. "I believe the quartermaster has asked for the floor first."

This diverted Jools's attention from his cavalry mates' shortcomings. The pale teenager opened a file on the laptop on the table in front of him. "You'll find on your network screens a diagram of the existing minecart tracks that serve the area, and my concept for a more thorough transit system."

The group viewed the shared file. On the map of abandoned tracks, Rob recognized the route that allied and syndicated griefers had used to cross biomes and haul loot. Their ruthless sieges on innocent villagers had brought Rob and company together to fight back.

Jools used his cursor as a pointer. "We already have track connecting Sunflower and Spike City via the extreme hills, through here. With a little maintenance, some spur tracks, and rail stations—here, here, and here—we'll have a complete loop suitable for passengers or freight. I suggest laying identical track alongside, so that traffic can move both ways at once."

Colonel M approved of the well-thought-out plan, but was quick to add a warning in his baritone voice: "This gives us an efficient supply route. It also creates an attractive target for griefers."

Jools put up a finger. "Way ahead of you, Colonel. We simply hire transport police to secure the railway, along with building and maintenance crews. Creation of jobs," he added, citing one of the city's main objectives for attracting citizens.

Artilleryman Stormie rose. "I second the colonel's motion. It'd be a heck of a luxury to ride the rails to distant biomes someday." The famed adventurer claimed to have already visited all of the Overworld territories in the course of her travels.

Rob frowned. "Cost analysis, please, Quartermaster."

Jools oversaw the cavalry's communal stores—which still included a vast amount of loot reappropriated from Bluedog, an unscrupulous moneylender they'd had dealings with. It was this fortune, along with Frida's substantial gift of jungle temple treasure, that would fund the city construction. Jools directed everyone's attention to columns of numbers that put his rail project well within their means.

"Public transit will cost money, but it will save money in the long run," he assured them.

They accepted the proposal and took up defense issues, eventually considering where to site a base camp and stable for the cavalry and their mounts. Corporal Kim, the company horse master, suggested a lush valley in the foothills, just a few minutes on foot from the city gates. Rob respected Kim's opinion and relied on her to care for, train, and outfit the battalion's herd—their most powerful weapon.

"We'll be wanting more horsepower, though," he said. "Incoming workers and travelers will need saddle and pack animals to go where the minecart system cannot reach."

"And we should have fresh mounts in our stable," tiny, pink-skinned Kim added. She pushed a pink leather cap back on her shiny black hair, causing her single golden earring to swing and catch the torchlight. "We've asked an awful lot of our horses," she said, "and so far, we've been lucky. I'd like to restart my breeding program at my farm on the sunflower plains—bring in a manager who can supply us with new horseflesh in Beta as we need it."

"Hear, hear, O bronc whisperer," Frida endorsed the measure, using the talented horse master's nickname.

"Seconded," Jools confirmed. His palomino stallion's deliberate manner wasn't always suited to hectic combat. Extra mounts would be appreciated. "I do love my Beckett, but from time to time a racehorse would come in handy."

Talk turned to iron golems, weapons, and the chain of command—all of which would be crucial in the city's defense. Colonel M offered to donate a pair of golems from those he had recently imported to guard his Nether fortress. Sergeant Turner, the resident weapons expert, ran down a long list of blades and other arms held in the company stockpile. His suggestion that he take over the battalion weapon inventories—"for safekeepin'"—was unanimously voted down.

"*Keeping,* perhaps," said Jools.

Stormie nodded. "*Safe,* not so much."

Turner had played fast and loose with company property one too many times. Rob only retained him as sergeant at arms for his intimate knowledge and application of weaponry.

Rob looked out the window of the shelter's conference room and saw that the shadows had grown long outside. The battalion had been here for hours debating the subject. He got up and placed an extra torch on the wall. "What's next, Judge?"

The jurist read from his agenda. "Section 2. What are the obstacles, and how shall we circumvent them?"

Everyone began talking at once:

"Bloodthirsty zombies!"

"Griefers'll steal our building supplies."

"Steal 'em? Heck, they'll bomb our supply lines."

"There could be an avalanche . . ."

"—a plague of silverfish . . ."

"—a terrible flood!"

The judge rapped the table with the flat of a wooden axe. "One at a time, people. One at a time!"

Colonel M added, "This matter may be critical to the success or failure of the project. Let us systematically discuss what might go wrong so we won't be blindsided."

Judge Tome backed up the colonel. "As we say in Latin, *Estote parati.* Be prepared, my friends. Or prepare for failure."

Rob filed this approach away for future reference. The judge was a master at analyzing the game. The colonel knew just how to lead players where he wanted them to go. He had once confided to the fledgling cavalry commander that he understood more about men than about strategy, but Rob suspected that the two elements were connected. The old war veteran had shown him that preparing his troopers in advance developed their respect, which was worth more in the heat of battle than all weaponry combined.

Darkness fell and the moans of mobs rose outside. The group continued to brainstorm until they'd considered every potential problem that could arise from every possible source—players, mobs, griefers, and even Mother Nature. They were busy debating viable workarounds when they heard a commotion outdoors.

"Uuuuhh . . . *ooohhh!*"

Glass shattered, and a mottled green arm thrust its way into the shelter. Turner, Frida, and Kim all lunged at it, blades clashing in their haste to sever the limb. Three more rotting arms poked through the opening, and this time the warriors took turns hacking them from the would-be intruders. The rising maggoty-meat stench made Rob gag.

Minus an arm, one of the zombies managed to crawl through the open block. Turner claimed the target, slashing at both of its legs. "Bet you always wanted to *travel!*" he growled, knocking the monster across the room, onto the table. The others drew back to let him work. "I'ma take you on a nice trip . . . to the *Nether,*" he shouted as he cut off the zombie's head and swiped the remaining mess onto the floor. He sheathed his weapon and dusted off his hands. Then he pulled a toothpick from behind his ear and casually worked at something between his teeth.

"I told De Vries, no windows!" Frida griped, chopping a dirt block from the floor and sealing off the gap in the wall.

Kim removed her cap and used it to gather the rotten flesh that had accumulated at their feet.

"Now, what were you saying, Stormie?" Frida asked, settling back down at the conference table as though nothing had happened.

Stormie picked some glass shards out of her long, curly black ponytail. "I think we can handle all threats from humans and hostiles. Avalanches are possible, but unlikely. Weather shouldn't be a problem at the altitude we've chosen for the city site."

"That just leaves the planning as a possible issue," Judge Tome concluded.

"I should say not!" Jools was offended. "I'm prepared to run through the blueprints, scheduling, and supply list with a fine-toothed comb. By the time I'm done, our construction program will be foolproof."

"*If* we're foolish enough to go through with it," Turner said, sitting back and lacing his fingers behind his dark buzz cut.

"Which brings us to our final matter." The judge stabbed a finger at the agenda, flashing his UBO ring. "Section 3. We agree that the concept has value and could hypothetically work. Are we willing to go through with it? We've come to the *yea* or *nay* vote."

Rob swallowed hard. It seemed that the interested parties could survive the building and running of a capital city. *But will they commit?* Battalion Zero's captain had faith in his troopers' individual strengths. However, he knew that getting these free spirits to unite as a group was like pulling mule teeth—tough, painful, and sometimes bloody.

"Let me summarize," boomed Colonel M in staccato bass tones. "*Yea* is yes to strengthening what remains of the United Biomes of the Overworld. Forming a capital city will give us one area to defend rather than worrying about multiple biome boundaries. A local police and standing army would augment the battalion's defense efforts. Having a physical seat of government will give villagers a concrete place to put their allegiance."

His expression grew more somber. "A *nay* vote disperses this committee and returns Overworld defense solely to the six of you."

Rob stood up and smoothed his leather vest and chaps. "It's a big job, folks. I won't lie about that. But banding the Overworld together'll let us go back to our normal lives, sooner or later. Letting it split further apart will only make life more difficult for everyone." He hoped this would sway his cavalry mates, each of whom had solid reasons for voting either way.

Judge Tome raised his eyeglasses and massaged the bridge of his nose. "If I might add . . . voting *yes* may revive democratic UBO governance. Voting *no* may kill it forever." He paused. "All in favor . . . ?"

Rob settled back in his chair, put up a hand, then held his breath. He knew Kim and Stormie wanted to return to their professions. Jools and Turner could surely make more money working for the GIA. And Frida—well, she'd called herself a lone wolf, shortly after they'd met. She might fade into the jungle and never be seen again.

First Kim's hand shot up. Then Stormie and Jools each raised a finger.

Rob looked at Frida. She nudged Turner, and then raised a hand.

Judge Tome hesitated, then asked, "All opposed...?"

"Hold on." Turner leaned forward and caught Rob's eye. "Pay's once a month?"

Rob found his voice. "Yes, yes!"

Turner raised two fingers. "I'm in, then."

The colonel and judge had already agreed to abide by the cavalry's decision, so the deal was done.

Rob made a pretend touchdown in the air and repeated, *"Yes!"*

"Way to go, Bat Zero!" cried Kim, raising a pink fist.

"Nothing like a vote for world peace," murmured Stormie. "Take *that*, Lady Craven." The deadly artillery expert had most recently struck a blow against the global security threat by the griefer alliance—and the sorcerer who commanded it.

Rob released a sigh, relieved that the vote had gone his way. "It'll be much easier to fend off Lady Craven and her legions from one citadel instead of chasing after them whenever and wherever they decide to strike."

"If they come back from Creative mode at all," Frida added. She'd been the one to change Lady Craven's game plan when the griefer queen's hordes had tried to enslave villagers in the Overworld's southern hemisphere.

Jools folded his arms. "If not them, it'll be some similar slimes."

"I like your faith in human nature," Rob said.

Turner grunted. "Some players always want more than they've got, and don't want to work for it."

Frida grinned at her old friend. "Unlike you. Right, Meat?"

Turner scowled. "Man's gotta make a livin'."

Judge Tome whacked the table with his axe again. "This is not the proper venue in which to discuss Sergeant Turner's moral conduct. *Alea iacta est.* The decision has been made." He smacked the table with his axe. "Meeting adjourned."

Rob got up and stretched, flooding with satisfaction as well as unease. The difficult debate was over. Now the real work of constructing a city and attracting residents and allies would begin. Then the players would have to stay alive long enough to institute a lawful government—all while keeping zombies, skeletons, creepers, and other assorted mobsters from interfering with the job. That was where Rob came in; the construction-phase defense would fall to his troopers.

That task would be an easy sell to the militant group. The real wild card would be how long he could count on their services.

But another tall order awaited them. The captain hadn't yet mentioned one more thing he'd require of his troops, and he wasn't quite sure how to bring it up. Faced with a tough decision, Turner and Frida could be volatile, and the others headstrong.

Rob would have to wait for his moment.

*

So, ground had been broken and the building begun. The cavalry set to crafting a horse camp and training ground—in between guarding workers and loot and taking out hostile mobs. As the days went by, though, Rob wondered about his ability to maintain his troops' commitment. Yes, they'd agreed to put their personal agendas on hold a while longer for the good of the Overworld. But for how long?

Once the first residents moved in, the city would be a prime target. Rob would need unquestioning loyalty from every member of Battalion Zero. Would he have it? As Rob let Stormie correct the spelling in his ad, he mused again about confronting his troops. He thought he'd come up with a way to ensure their unity . . . but they might not like it.

The situation reminded him of his first night in the Overworld, after falling from the airplane into the ocean. His unexpected swim had left him with next to nothing: no food, no weapons, and barely the clothes on his back. His cowboy hat had been lost in the surf. When Rob finally washed up on the beach, all he'd had for protection was a pillar of sand—and he didn't know whether it would hold together, or disintegrate into a billion tiny pieces.

CHAPTER 2

THE CLOSER THE DATE CAME TO WELCOMING NEW residents to Beta, the more misgivings Captain Rob had about the battalion's ability to safeguard the city. He'd already called for daily training and confined the troopers to the area 24/7. But since his "moment" had never come, he still hadn't mentioned his final service requirement.

"That does it! Today's the day," he said to himself. He'd learned from the disastrous events leading up to the Battle of Zombie Hill that action—however unrehearsed—must ultimately trump caution. But preparation, he recalled the judge saying, might help keep him and his troops alive.

Rob walked across the valley compound to where the others were fortifying the stable area. Their horses were fit and fleet—except for slow-moving Beckett, who had other virtues. The mounts would be targets for griefers and malcontents, not to mention creepers and wolves.

A permanent barn shelter had yet to be built, so the horses were being watched closely outdoors. A wide, torch-lit pasture lay not far from the company bunkhouse, across a patch of ground that had been cleared and its dirt blocks swept clean. The captain's approach was heralded with a long, low whinny from his warhorse, Saber, and a high-octave bray from Norma Jean, the talkative mule that belonged to Judge Tome. She punctuated her greeting by raising her tail and emitting three farts. Rob gave her a good-natured salute.

Eight more rumps and tails were all that could be seen of the other animals, which did not lift their heads from the rich grass they dined on. Surrounding the herd was a typically fenced pasture ringed by an atypical ditch. It was several blocks deep and wide and—thus far—empty. A trip wire encircled the field, and the stream that naturally ran through it had been dammed. Water pooled in a small pond outside the fence. Rob was pleased with the way the accommodations were shaping up.

"First part's all done, Cap'n," Turner said, rubbing his palms together. Sweat glued the mercenary's ripped T-shirt to his torso and trickled across the mesa and desert biome tattoos on his biceps. His cargo pants and combat boots were crusted with dirt.

"I'm glad to see you're not above a little ditch digging, Sergeant."

"Oh, we did that with a modified power shovel. I was just lifting some weights." Turner stepped back to reveal a massive iron barbell resting on a rack above a bench press he'd crafted. "Want to have a go? I'll spot you."

"Er, no, thanks." The sergeant's muscles had muscles, while Rob's physique was more . . . streamlined—better for jumping on and off a cowhorse in his world. Rob had made it a policy never to lift anything heavier than himself.

Turner shook his head. "Strong get stronger and the weak get weaker," he muttered.

"What's next for the ditch?" Rob asked, changing the subject. "It might trap a zombie, but a skeleton or a human could get in and out pretty easy."

Jools, sitting with the others nearby, heard him talking and came over. "Not to worry, Captain." He motioned to Kim, Frida, and Stormie, who were sharpening the ends of stout saplings with iron axes. "We fill the trench with hundreds of these Punji sticks, like so—" He jumped down into the gully and pantomimed jamming a stake upright in the ground. He squinted up at Rob. "Then we open the irrigation gates and flood the thing. There'll be a drawbridge for us to get in and out."

"A booby-trapped moat?"

"Brilliant, if I say so, myself. First the bad guys fall, then they're skewered, then they drown." Jools reached for the ledge to pull himself back out again.

Rob gave him a hand. "Sounds like overkill to me."

"Nothin' wrong with that!" Turner praised.

"Oh, I agree." Rob stood back and admired the design. "The more work the traps do, the less work for us."

Turner considered this and then corrected him. "Fightin' ain't near work, Cap'n. More like a hobby than anything else." He turned and dove at Frida, who dropped the stake she was sharpening just in time to deflect the full-body blow.

They wrestled in the dirt for a bit, Turner raking at Frida's short, dark hair, and Frida biting any extremity her teeth could get ahold of. Turner got up and began pelting her with rocks. Enraged, the survivalist tensed her muscles and then uncoiled, rolling toward the mercenary's feet. His boots flew out from under him, and he fell heavily into the empty pit. Rob thought he felt the ground shake.

After a slight pause, Turner crawled out of the dry moat and staggered over to Frida, grabbing her hand in a sideways clasp and releasing it. "You're one up on me," he complimented her.

"Too bad I hadn't placed those spikes yet," murmured Jools.

"All right, all right," Rob said, to cover his admiration for Frida's combat skill. There was something thrilling about a woman who could fight like that. "If you folks want to spar, let's get mounted. You can finish the moat later."

Battalion Zero's main advantage against hostiles and griefers was its ability to fight together as a cavalry unit. The captain made an effort to keep the troopers' skills sharp. He had to admit that—what with the conferences and the guarding and the crafting—their horsemanship had slipped somewhat.

Kim produced the horses' inventory, and the group climbed over the trip wire, through the ditch, and into the pasture to tack up. Rob recognized an opportunity for a teaching moment. "Troops! Once we're mounted, I want us all to jump this moat once in each direction." Who knew if some griefer might succeed in disabling the drawbridge? Planning an alternate means of escape now could save lives.

"No fair!" Jools complained. "You've got Pegasus. I've got a four-toed sloth."

A corner of Rob's mouth turned up. It was well known that Saber loved to jump, while Beckett practically needed a potion of leaping to do so.

"What is it Judge Tome says about practice making perfect, Quartermaster?"

"*Usus magister est optimus.* But in this case, it only makes me a perfect prat."

Jools knew better than to argue with an order, though. He saddled his palomino stallion and took his position in file behind Duff, Turner's blocky gray quarter horse.

Stormie began the exercise on her brave black-and-white paint horse, Armor. Frida took advantage of Armor's momentum by following closely on Ocelot, the black-and-brown spotted pony she rode. In and out they sprang, before Turner or Jools had encouraged Duff or Beckett to jump one way.

Rob eyed Kim, who had mounted Nightwind, the huge bay stallion that Colonel M had bequeathed to her. She nodded.

"Follow us!" Rob called, as he led the way on Saber. This example worked, and the others completed the drill, with Saber throwing in a pair of extra leaps for good measure. Rob patted the horse's shiny black neck, thinking how lucky he was to have found an equal to Pistol, his versatile horse back on the ranch in his old life.

Then it was time for the group to get down to business. "Troops, fall in!" Captain Rob ordered, and the riders arranged their mounts as usual: Armor first, then Ocelot, then Duff, Beckett, Nightwind, and Saber.

The fenced pasture made an ideal arena for performing the mounted patterns that allowed the cavalry to function as a group when traveling or skirmishing. The six horse-and-rider pairs could move together in single file, by twos, or split into two separate lines. They practiced circling, turning, and moving at, and away from, each other at a walk, trot, and gallop. Not only were these maneuvers efficient ways to get where they were going or sidle up to the enemy—they also looked super cool. The normally safe workout, however, turned dangerous when the timing of any single rider was off. And the timing was off today.

They were engaged in a simple, single-file trot when Frida let Ocelot get too close to Armor's rump. Armor took this as an insult and kicked out at the mare's face, barely missing it. This stopped up the line and created a multi-horse pileup that dealt iron-shod damage all around, as each animal retaliated with a kick.

They took a short break so that Jools could distribute healing potions. Then they resumed . . . but their performance didn't improve.

When they split into two groups and rode at each other, trying to thread through the oncoming file, glancing blows left three riders on the ground and three horses' shoulders in need of a rubdown. And—although it was nobody's fault—a bee sting transformed placid Beckett into an uncontrollable projectile that threatened to unseat the riders who *hadn't* fallen off yet.

"Say, Jools, maybe you've found Beckett's incentive for jumping!" called Kim as the quartermaster screamed his way across the field atop the bucking Beckett.

Rob reined Saber over to the agitated pair and edged the palomino into the fence, ending the show. Still, every mount jigged or pulled at the reins in an attempt to work off the tension, much to the chagrin of their riders. Trying to find a good note to end on might get someone seriously hurt. And Rob wasn't about to start an armed drill in this atmosphere.

"Is it too late to form a dismounted unit?" Jools asked.

"Don't worry. We'll give it another shot tomorrow," Rob announced. "Let's walk up to the construction site. It might give us some ideas for improving defense."

*

The contractor met them at the temporary city gate, where two of Colonel M's iron golems were leashed.

"S'up, Crash?" Stormie greeted the young woman who was overseeing the building.

The short, stocky player was dressed in a protective leather suit and cap. Sandy hair framed her squarish face, and her fair skin looked as though sunlight rarely touched it. She waved her diamond pickaxe at the guards, and they let the foot soldiers pass through the makeshift chainmail fence.

Once inside, Crash doled out a half dozen protective helmets just like her own—stiff, yellow leather with redstone-powered headlamps attached to the fronts.

"Always wanted one o' these," Turner said enthusiastically, tugging his on.

Crash fixed him with a glare.

"They're loaners, Meat," Frida translated. "Safety first."

"Nice to see you, Private," Rob said to Crash. The contractor and her brother had ridden with Battalion Zero during the previous campaign. They'd been pressed into service on the Beta project to take advantage of their architectural prowess. Rob knew that mining building materials was Crash's passion and area of expertise. "We'd love a tour of the foundation and any . . . secret passageways we should know about."

Jools sidled up. "Nothing like an escape hatch, I always say." He had been instrumental in reviewing the city's building design and making sure there were no loose ends.

Crash opened a laptop she was carrying and brought up the working blueprints to show him.

"Get some screenshots, will you, Quartermaster?" Rob asked, breaking away to look around the grounds.

To the uninformed eye, the site resembled a battle-field that had seen recent action. Trees lay blackened, uprooted, and tossed aside. The earth bore scars from restless pickaxes and heavy machinery. A handful of leather-clad workers marching through the lot might as easily have been carrying bodies as building blocks. Portions of a boundary wall, a grand capitol, and a variety of household dwellings rose, half-formed, from the stripped ground. These could well have been either bombed-out remnants or works-in-progress. A jobsite trailer and stone conference hall were the only completed structures.

Crash cut off Rob's questions about them by raising a horizontal palm above her head and hooking a thumb in the direction of the office trailer. Her taller brother, De Vries, would have the answers. De Vries, the lead architect, was known for his lavish interiors and exteriors. Crash, though, was more interested in the work belowground. Even now, she chopped and stacked cobblestone, pockmarking the path along which they walked.

The zealous miner led the group past the city center and into a cavern where the growing citadel was set into the cliffside. The site had been chosen for its protection by the towering extreme hills, as well as for the ores that they contained. Much of the building material could be mined directly from the caves and player-made tunnels.

"This place gives me the creeps," Stormie confided to Frida as they walked into a many-armed cavern. It lay very near the spot where the adventurer had lost her life in the epic Zombie Hill battle.

Frida squeezed her arm. "That'll pass once De Vries has dolled it up. You'll see."

They descended a stone walkway lined with torches, its walls cratered with half-dug stores of coal, iron, emerald, and gold. A spur track alongside the incline allowed the minerals to be hauled to the surface by minecart. One of these vehicles spilled over with lapis and diamond blocks.

"Lookit the loot!" exclaimed Turner.

"Impressive," Rob said.

"Certainly cuts down on the materials overhead," Jools remarked.

Crash tugged on the sleeve of Rob's western-style shirt and increased her pace, taking a dirt-floored corridor that branched off to the left and farther downward. She motioned for the others to lift torches from the wall to carry with them.

The dots of light were not enough, though, to prevent mobs from spawning. Two baby zombies crawled quickly up the slope toward them on rotting hands and knees. "Guuuuhh . . . *gaaahhh*!" came their high-pitched moans.

The sound of six iron swords being drawn sliced through the air.

Kim motioned the others aside. "Allow me," she called. "I love kids."

Crash and Rob let the horse master pass to charge at the treacherous tykes. She'd had it in for the undead ever since her horses had been zombified by Lady Craven's predecessor, Dr. Dirt.

Kim flew at the mobsters with her naked blade, her arm a blur in the half light. "Didn't your mommies teach you not to play in the *dirt*?" she taunted as she borrowed from Turner's playbook, striking the zombie babies in quick succession. They expired, dropping several brand-new shovels before they disappeared.

Crash smacked her forehead with a palm and went to collect the tools.

"Equipment went missing?" Stormie guessed.

Jools muttered, "Typical construction site."

Crash stowed the shovels in an idle minecart and resumed her tour. At last, they reached a circular underground room that made several of the visitors catch their breath.

Lit by a stagnant lava pool at one end, a square stone dungeon was clearly visible within the vast space. Enormous red and brown mushrooms sprang from the floor and walls, amid thick veins of redstone ore.

Rob stared. "Good griefer! Is this what I think it is?"

Turner muscled his way to the front. "You're darn tootin'. This room alone is worth a fortune!" He turned to Crash. "Does anyone else know about this?"

She shook her head.

Kim, Frida, and Stormie caught up with the rest of the group. The artilleryman waved at the dungeon. "Can we take a peek inside? Might be some gunpowder in there I could use."

"Or some horse armor or golden apples," Kim said hopefully.

Crash swept an arm open, in invitation.

They started for the structure, but Frida stopped them. The vanguard considered it her duty to scout out danger. "Let me search for monster eggs first. Might be where the zombies came from." As her work boot touched the porch steps, though, an ominous rumbling filled the cavern.

The next second, the stone beneath Frida's feet gave way. She screamed.

Rob watched in horror as the entire dungeon sank rapidly away, the vanguard sliding after it, clutching at the air with her hands. She managed to hook four fingers on the ragged edge of the hole and dangled in midair.

"H-help me!" Her free arm waved wildly, causing her fingers to slip.

Rob started for the opening, but Turner leapt toward it first. "Hang on, pal!" He dropped to his stomach at the edge and leaned farther over than gravity would seem to allow, groping for Frida's free hand. The movement knocked her grip loose.

"Turner!" she screamed.

"I gotcha," he said, grabbing her around the waist before she could fall, but now teetering with the extra weight.

Rob's heart jumped into his throat, and his stomach plunged to his feet. Then he heard a chopping sound, and Turner's prone body stabilized. Crash had pinned his pants to solid ground with her pickaxe.

"Quick thinking, Private," Rob said, hustling up to grab Turner's ankles.

Jools joined him, and together they pulled Turner and Frida to safety. Frida gave Rob a grateful glance. It was all the captain could do not to cradle her in his arms.

"Let's get out of here!" Stormie cried, making an about face and not stopping to wait for them.

Back on the surface, the friends stood at the mouth of the cavern, trying to regain their composure.

"That was close," Turner acknowledged, poking his finger through the hole that Crash had ripped in his pants.

Frida balled her fist in pain where her fingernails had broken off.

"A flipping sinkhole!" Jools said. "That's a death trap if there ever was one. I about had kittens, and I was nowhere near it."

Rob's guts sloshed like stormy seas. *If anything had happened to Frida . . .*

He put a hand on Crash's elbow. "Has something like this gone down before?"

She hesitated, then dipped her head.

"What? How many times?" Frida pressed.

Crash held up five fingers.

"Dang," Stormie said.

Rob moaned. "Why wasn't I informed? Could be every inch of this site is structurally unsound!"

"But the data says otherwise. . . ." Jools argued.

"Might not *be* unsound." Stormie's dusky face showed suspicion. "Could be someone wants us to think it is."

*

The incident illustrated the need for Rob to have a candid talk with his troopers. Clearly, the Beta project was in jeopardy. Frida and Turner had nearly died. And if they had, they could have respawned anywhere. They'd shared their origins with no one, and could get lost in the Nether or pop up in some distant biome where they couldn't be traced. Rob knew the moment had come.

After dinner that night, as the battalion sat around the campfire, he got their attention. "Listen up, folks. Before we go any farther with this city thing, I have a request."

"More cake?" Kim asked, offering him seconds of dessert.

He thanked her, but declined. "It's more serious than that." He got to his feet. He'd rehearsed his speech many times. "As your captain, your safety is of the utmost importance to me. Consider that we are now in a position to influence Overworld history. Each one of you—and me, too—is crucial to the success of the free world."

They murmured a bit, Turner elbowing Frida. "Told ya I was indispensable."

"Indispensable, yes," Rob echoed. "Also . . . unfortunately, human and expendable. Today showed us that. It's a dangerous business we're in, and at any turn, any one of us could—"

Stormie beat him to the punch. "Die." She raised a hand. "Done that, sir."

Frida reached over and squeezed her shoulder.

"Yes," Rob said, his throat tightening. He tried to mask his feelings. "And we were incredibly lucky to have met up with you again." He took a deep breath.

"When Colonel M talked to us about planning ahead for contingencies, it got me thinking. What if one or more of us dies and *doesn't* respawn within range? What if we're in the middle of battle or at a critical stage in a mission?"

Kim understood. "It could doom the rest of us."

"The rest of us—heck, it could mean villagers' lives," Stormie replied.

"And once the biomes are united, every corner of the Overworld could be left unprotected," Frida said.

Turner grunted. "Hey. Not sayin' we ain't great fighters, but, beggin' the captain's pardon, we hardly got tabs on the whole Overworld."

Rob reclaimed the floor. "You all took on this job *because* the whole world's future is at stake." He looked at Turner. "Because you care. Whether it's the people or their pocketbooks you're interested in, you *do* care."

Jools piped up, "So, what is it you want of us, Captain? Not to die? I am so on board with that."

Rob didn't smile. "We can't control if we die. But we can control where we're reborn."

Now everyone figured out where their leader's speech was heading. The joking stopped.

Rob said solemnly, "I'm invoking my authority as commander of this unit to ask everyone here to change their spawn points to Beta, effective immediately."

This stunned the group silent.

Frida's and Turner's spawn points had always been kept strictly secret, according to their survivalist codes. Jools and Stormie had died and respawned so many times that they never intended to let that happen again, ever. And Kim and Rob wanted to avoid both dying and respawning elsewhere, so they'd be able to see to the horses—either here, or on Rob's alternate worldly plane.

"I know it's asking a lot. . . ." Rob said.

Turner shot him a look. "You askin'? Or tellin'?"

"Consider it a mandatory request. Can I have your word?"

No one replied.

Rob sighed. *I was afraid of that.* He'd have to play his only remaining card. "I'll withhold your pay until I get an answer, then."

CHAPTER 3

THAT NIGHT, THE INTERIOR OF THE BUNKHOUSE, which De Vries and his crew had built for the battalion, was uncharacteristically quiet. Rob made ready to turn in, fully intending to sleep in a real bed for the first time in this version of the world. He'd been making do with a woolen bedroll, which suited him fine but wouldn't change his spawn point.

He removed his vest and boots, the reality of what was about to happen foremost in his mind. "Can't ask my troops to do anything I won't do," he said to himself. If he didn't uphold his end of the bargain, he'd gain neither compliance nor respect from the cavalry team, and he was skating on thin ice already.

The clamor of skeletons and zombies rose to its customary level outside as Rob spread his bedroll on the handsome wooden cot that De Vries had crafted.

How he wished he could swap the lowing of cattle and crackle of a dwindling campfire for the monsters' din. If he were back home, he'd be sleeping under the stars with his old dog, Jip, curled beside him, anticipating another peaceful day of riding fences. The air would smell of sweet, wild sage and of hearty coffee waiting in the pot for tomorrow's breakfast.

He pulled back the bedroll. Once he slept in a proper bed there'd be no way to return to his entry point into the Overworld. Rob hadn't had the presence of mind to fix that spot in his memory as he tumbled from the aircraft into the ocean, or as he swam for his life toward an unseen shore. When he hit the beach, his only thoughts were for survival. By the time he wondered where he was, it was too late to recall where he had actually been at that critical moment in time. Something had gone wrong with the plane, but he had never found out what it was or what had become of the other passengers.

He'd thought he was alone on an island—until Frida trapped him and gave him the third degree, trying to find out whether or not he was a griefer. Although he and Frida had since grown close, Rob never forgot that he was far from home. And he had never felt farther away from it than he did right now.

He stared at the bed a moment longer. He could still hike up to the tip of the extreme hills to try to spy the place where he'd entered the ocean or made it to shore. That had been his intention before the Battle of Zombie Hill, when he and his cavalry mates were forced to retreat through the Nether, or die trying to hold the clifftop. The stakes in this game were always so high.

Rob grabbed the edge of the bedroll decisively and yanked it off the bed. *I can't! I just—can't. Not yet.*

He settled on top of the soft fleece stretched across the plank floor next to the bed. It took a very long time to fall asleep that night.

*

Then it seemed as though dawn would never come. To avoid placing windows, at Frida's request, De Vries had devised a light-level monitor using sugarcane tubing, mirrors, and a pinhole through the roof. Rob awoke several times and checked this "periscope" for daylight, without success. Then he finally fell into a deep sleep when it was nearly time to get up, so he missed seeing dawn's early light. A rattle on his door woke him.

"Sorry, Captain," came Frida's voice. "Your meeting at Beta is set in half an hour. You're supposed to ride out afterwards."

Rob sat up on his bedroll, dazed, until he remembered what had gone wrong the night before. Then he scrambled to his feet, slipped into his vest and boots, and exited his quarters. An officer couldn't dwell on his mistakes.

Rob entered the bunkhouse's common room, where the others were filling their food bars.

"Late night, sir?" Stormie asked. He shrugged.

Kim brought him some bread and pork chops. "Morning, Captain! You're going to need this."

Rob had asked for an emergency consult with Colonel M, Judge Tome, and the builder regarding the sinkhole episode. Afterwards, he planned to take a squadron out to the sunflower and ice plains to connect with their new UBO delegates in the villages. So far, they had enlisted the two biomes as allies, and they had put in requests to a dozen more. While on the plains, the squadron would look in on Kim's horse breeding operation.

"Pack some rations for the road trip, will you, Corporal?"

Kim nodded, excitement lighting her pink face. "I can't wait to see my horses. Thank you for letting me get the farm squared away. I'm sure Swale will do a good job." She had hired a dirt-poor farmer they knew who could use the job and who was a solid hand with horses. "I was so relieved to have someone capable there," she added, "that I went ahead and changed my spawn point last night." She grinned. "Slept like a baby zombie."

Rob tried to cover the shame that seeped through him. "How about the rest of you?" he asked the others gruffly.

Jools swallowed some breakfast and looked up from his computer. "I'm still weighing the pros and cons."

"Me, too," said Stormie, turning away from the captain.

There was a pause.

"Frida?" Rob prompted.

Another pause.

"Thinking about it," she mumbled.

Rob faced Turner. *"Well?"*

The sergeant scowled. "Uh . . . thinkin' about thinking about it."

"You do that."

Rob took Jools and Frida with him to meet the others at Beta. Today, Crash's brother, De Vries, met them at the gate. He passed out yellow helmets.

"Can't be too careful!" the builder remarked in his lilting voice. In addition to his cap, De Vries sported the safari-style jacket and clogs that both he and Crash had favored when they'd traveled with the battalion in months past. He led them to the office, where the colonel and judge waited.

Rob asked Jools to show the others the screenshots of the building blueprints Crash had sent. They compared these to a detailed map of the terrain crafted by Stormie and a rough sketch of the cavern where the sinkhole had opened up. Next, they plotted the other known sinkhole occurrences on the map but found nothing clear that might have caused them. The natural cave network did not appear vulnerable to collapse, and Crash had taken pains to mine the tunnels sustainably.

De Vries said, "We've been over and over the specs. The margin for error was miniscule. This ground's stable."

"Which makes an outside influence more likely," Jools said.

"A mole?" Rob asked.

Colonel M pursed his large lips. "Maybe a human one."

Frida considered this. "Someone knew exactly where to open up a tunnel to get at that dungeon. No telling what all was in there."

Judge Tome spoke up: "Anyone after a monster spawner or loot is probably not the sort of colonist we're seeking. Speaking of which"—he pushed a stack of papers toward Frida—"I believe these are for you."

She read the heading on the top sheet: "'Residency Application.' These are from people who answered the ad?"

There were dozens of them. Rob always tried to put his troopers' strengths to good use, and he knew the survivalist could read players like a book. Frida had been tagged to sort through the applications and reject any unsavory prospects.

"You'll work on those while our squadron is off on its mission, Corporal." Rob turned to the colonel and judge. "Do you have anything for me to deliver to our delegates?"

The judge produced a copy of the charter they'd drafted and some paperwork for the new liaisons to fill out.

"De Vries," Rob said, "lock down those blueprints. We can't have any more leaks."

"You might want to change the access codes," Jools suggested.

Rob hated to leave town now that the project—and his friends—seemed to be at risk. "I'll be back in a few days. Call Turner if you need help."

As the meeting broke up, Rob asked Colonel M for a private word. Impressed by Rob's pluck when he had first formed the cavalry unit, the old ghost had taken him under his wing. The senior officer had a great deal of wisdom to impart, having seen so much action in the years leading up to the First War.

"What can I do for you, Captain?"

"It has to do with my command, sir."

Colonel M gave a low chuckle. "I don't envy you. Your troopers are strong-willed enough to triumph, yet stubborn enough to drive you mad."

Rob stared at the floor. "It's me that's the trouble this time." He would rather not broach the subject, but managed to share his moral dilemma with his mentor.

"I see," Colonel M said when Rob had finished.

"I know enough not to ask more of my troops than I'm prepared to give myself. I'm just . . . not ready to give it." He started pacing. "I *know* how important it is for the battalion to stick together. But if I change my spawn point, I might never find my way home." Rob cast inquiring eyes on the colonel. "What should I do?"

The colonel knit his enormous brow and thought a moment. Personal matters fell into a gray area where he rarely meddled. Finally, he said, "I cannot tell a man how to act. I can, however, tell you what to consider. First, I will need to know more about how the enlistees have received your . . . mandatory request."

They discussed each trooper's background and response to the order to change spawn points. Then they talked a bit about Rob's old life and the commitments he'd made in the course of his work there. The colonel wanted to know if some prior experience might guide the cowboy-turned-cavalry-commander. Had he put himself on the line for the good of others in the past?

Rob had, during his range duties, faced all kinds of dangers. He told the colonel he'd suffered rattlesnake bites and barbed-wire cuts, wolf attacks and cattle stampedes. But he'd never quit—never refused to ford a stream to save a calf, never hesitated to brave quicksand to save a cow.

"Why?" Colonel M asked. "Why did you persist?"

Rob searched his soul. "I . . . don't know why."

The colonel gave him a long look. "Come back and talk to me again when you do."

Rob excused himself, no closer to finding the grit necessary to change his spawn point. Still, he felt buoyed by the idea that his old life held the key to resolving his present worries. And, even though he'd admitted his shameful failure, the colonel had treated him as though trying and failing were part of honorably fulfilling his duty.

Maybe it's a process, and not a permanent flaw, he thought. In any case, he had certainly improved from his early days as a commander. Rob felt that he might, one day, have the strength do his captain's bars justice.

*

A short while later, Rob, Jools, and Kim mounted up and guided their horses down through the foothills, following the abandoned minecart tracks to the northwest. They soon crossed the biome border into Bryce Mesa, where the cavalry had once encamped to prepare for battle with the griefers' mob army. The successful strategy had produced one of the battalion's most rousing victories.

The horses' shod feet clapped loudly against the hardened clay and the sun beat down on the travelers' backs. "There's our old camp!" Kim cried happily as the three troopers rode past a red-orange cliff lined with striped hoodoo spires and bright-green cacti.

Rob recalled seeing this country for the first time. The high desert terrain, with its imposing sandstone towers and long, dry stretches broken by bubbling streams was not so different from his home rangeland. His conversation with Colonel M drifted back, driving Rob so deeply into thought that, to get his attention, Jools had to poke him with the stick he carried to rouse Beckett.

The captain about jumped out of his skin. "What? What?"

"Just wondering if you know of a village in these parts. It would be capital if this biome joined the UBO, don't you think? Fond memories here."

Rob grinned. "Likewise. I'll have to check with Frida and Stormie. They're on outreach detail. Tell you what, though: if there aren't any sizeable settlements, we'll seed one and you can move in—once the Overworld's secure, that is."

"Smashing, sir."

The sun crossed its high point in the cloudless sky, and the party left mesa clay behind. The horses dove eagerly into the sea of grass and cheerful flowers common to the plains variant. Friendly cows and pigs trundled alongside them safely, as the troopers carried plenty to eat. When a string of wild mustangs ran by in the distance, Rob felt his blood pump a bit harder.

Before too long the riders approached Sunflower, the village that lay not far from Kim's horse farm. While still fifty blocks off, they could see a white-clad form waving at them from the parapet of the town wall.

Jools pointed. "It must be Aswan!"

When they got closer, they could make out the apron and earnest features of the village leather worker, a man who was a canny trader and a special admirer of Kim's. The three friends dismounted and led their horses through the gate. Rob was glad to see that the war-torn village had managed to craft a new iron golem.

"Oh, Kim—beautiful flower, light of my life!" Aswan hailed Battalion Zero's horse master from his perch. "Do not fade. I'll be right down!"

Jools and Rob looked at each other. Kim took the compliments in stride, as usual. While they waited, she waved and nodded to residents she knew.

The leather worker appeared and took Nightwind's reins from Kim. "You're like a ray of sunshine on a stormy day," he said to her fervently.

"The better to keep the skellies away," Jools quipped.

Kim smiled noncommittally.

"Delegate," Rob greeted him. "We're right pleased you'll be working with us." The tradesman's intelligence network had helped the battalion deal with griefers in the past.

Now Aswan grinned, revealing several of his gold teeth. "It's one way to stay in the know."

"I'm sure it will be a two-way street."

Aswan nodded in Kim's direction. "If only it were a honeymoon suite." When she didn't react, he said, "But, you must be hungry! And tired, of course. Come along. Let's get you settled for the night." He noticed a creeper spawn up ahead, moving in their direction, so he steered Nightwind away.

Jools pulled a bow and arrows from his inventory. *P-rong! P-rong!* The creeper imploded and dropped a bit of gunpowder, which a wayward village child snatched and ran off with before anyone else could get to it.

On their way down the main village street, the troopers paused to do some trading. Jools popped in to visit the librarian, to get some glass he needed for crafting brewing bottles. Then he and Aswan waited at the village well while Kim and Rob visited Sundra, the blacksmith and armorer. She reset Nightwind's shoes and repaired some chainmail boots Rob had acquired from a skeleton drop. Sundra, who was sweet on the battalion's sergeant at arms, asked after Turner's health. She followed the troopers outside to say hello to Jools, who had also caught her eye during previous trades.

"You're looking smart, Sundra," Jools complimented the sturdily built woman. "Is that a new hairstyle?"

"Naw," she said, preening bashfully, "I've dyed it!" Her long, straight hair was now the same reddish color of her skin.

"It suits you," Rob said, causing her to flush an even deeper shade of red and flutter her eyelashes at him hopefully. He tried to redirect her interest. "Sorry Turner couldn't ride out with us this time."

"You tell that beefsteak of a man my barn door's always open," she said.

They took their leave and headed for Aswan's shop and home. Rob felt a warm glow spread through his chest. It felt good to see acquaintances in a part of the Overworld he'd visited before. It made him feel less like a stranger in a strange land, and more like . . . he belonged.

The group arrived at Aswan's fortified bunker, where they saw to the horses and presented a few leather goods that needed mending or modifying. While the tradesman worked on a pair of shoulder holsters for Turner, the troopers filled their food bars with fresh produce. Aswan also produced three cakes for dessert—one for each of them. Kim's had been decorated with frosting flowers and an outline of a heart with an arrow through it.

"Sweets for the sweet," Aswan murmured when she expressed her thanks.

After their appetites were satisfied and the repair work done, their host managed to shelve his feelings for Kim long enough to sit down and discuss UBO business. "Now, can you tell me in detail what my delegate duties will be?" he asked. "I want to do all I can to promote a righteous government."

The village of Sunflower had been targeted again and again by the griefer army, which had threatened, pillaged, and burned out the inhabitants in an effort to take over the plains biome. But the villagers had fought back, first in a battle to protect their own territory, and later, for the good of the Overworld in the failed attempt at Zombie Hill. When approached with the prospect of a resurrected UBO administration, Aswan had rallied the villagers in support. They'd selected him as their biome delegate.

"The colonel and judge are finalizing plans for democratic input," Rob informed Aswan. "For now, you'll be invited to bring your village's concerns to the table and enlist volunteers for civic duties."

Jools helped the new ambassador set up a secure network connection for online meetings of the governing body. In exchange for his participation and a small monthly sum in trade from the villagers, the United Biome administration would provide defense—by the cavalry in the short term, and by the standing army once it got on its feet. Rob's leadership was held in high regard throughout the village. Some of the Sunflowerites had expressed interest in joining up.

"We could use your help with another matter, too," Rob told Aswan.

The three troopers related the sinkhole incident and their suspicion that griefers might be targeting the capital city's construction. "Can you sniff out any news of gang activity in our area?" Rob asked the leather worker. "We're interested in someone who might be operating underground."

"And keep it under your helmet," Kim added. "We don't want anyone to suspect that the UBO might be in trouble."

"I should say, Delegate, this is right up your street," Jools put in. They all knew that the tradesman was a master at keeping an ear to the ground while maintaining a firmly buttoned lip.

Aswan flashed all of his gold teeth this time. "You can count on me."

CHAPTER 4

THE TRADESMAN BADE KIM AND COMPANY A tearful farewell when they set out the next morning for her farm. "Don't forget to write!" he called as Kim waved good-bye from Nightwind's back.

The mood was far lighter on their approach to Kim's property than it had been the last time, when the specter of zombie horses awaited them. Rob felt his heart skip a beat at the sight of the farm's well-kept fencing and horses up to their hocks in thick grass. *That's the way it should be,* he thought, wishing the battalion's herd didn't require a booby-trapped moat to keep them safe.

The group found Swale in his vegetable patch near the stable. The man's prospects had improved considerably, and it showed. His unkempt hair had been trimmed, his clothing was neat, and he proudly showed them boxes of healthy seedlings bound for Beta city. The Overworld capital was to have its own irrigated garden alongside the community well, to serve its residents.

"Here's them melon and pumpkin starts you asked for," he said, and Jools placed them in his inventory for transport. Swale turned to Kim. "Now, I have a surprise for you."

He led them to a large stall in the stable that was bedded heavily with sweet-smelling straw. When Rob's vision adjusted to the dimness, he saw two pairs of soft doe-eyes looking back at them.

"Josie!" Kim cried, moving swiftly for the door. "And . . . a little Josie!" She slid the stall door open and let herself in. A copper-colored mare and her fuzzy foal stood their ground, and the baby stretched out its neck in Kim's direction. Then the little thing jumped straight up in the air, lost its footing, and landed in a heap.

"She's a firecracker," Swale said, smiling. "And a big, strong filly. What'll you name her?"

Kim turned to Rob and Jools. "Any ideas?"

"She'll likely be chestnut colored, like her mama," Rob said.

"How about Redstone?" Jools suggested.

"Full of energy," Kim said. "That's it!"

They admired the filly a bit longer and then strode out to the pastures to see the saddle horse prospects that Swale was training. Rob ached to handle them—just give up being captain for a day and enjoy the way time unraveled when working with horses. But Swale was new to the job and clearly proud of what he'd accomplished so far. Rob didn't want to steal his thunder.

Coincidentally, a sound like thunder arose as they stood observing one of the young horses. Hoof beats indicated somebody moving in from the north.

Rob and the others cast worried gazes at the horizon and saw a party of three riders skirting a distant stand of trees. They were too far off to identify, and they kept going on past until they were out of sight again.

Swale frowned at the breach in countryside etiquette. "Friendlies would've visited."

"Uglies would've attacked," Jools said.

"Unless they saw us and felt outnumbered," Kim argued.

Rob had noted the absence of security measures on the place. "Swale, how're you fixed for weapons?" he asked.

The simple farmer cocked his head. "I've got plenty of hoe and shovel handles, if that's what you mean."

Rob caught Kim's eye. The two troopers had first met the farmer when rustlers made off with some of his herd. "Corporal. Why don't you craft some weapons and give Mr. Swale, here, some instruction in using them? Jools and I will make the trek to Spike City and meet you back at Beta. Oh, and tame a couple of wolves. Let's keep Josie and Redstone safe."

*

Rob and Jools set out right away for the long ride over the extreme hills to the ice plains. A double potion of swiftness perked up Beckett's gait to match Saber's energetic trot. The cavalry troopers followed the old minecart route back toward Beta. They stopped briefly to check in with Stormie, Frida, and Turner, who were holding down the fort.

Seeing that the cav camp was in order and hearing that construction was moving along, the captain and quartermaster continued on their journey, up and over the mountainous summit. On their way down the other side, Rob pointed out the Nether portal that lay near the site of their last horrific battle with Lady Craven's mobs. He couldn't help but picture the scene he'd witnessed that night, full of monsters and destruction. The hillside had been ablaze, the air thick with smoke—as though the Overworld had traded places with the Nether.

"I'd never seen so many zombies," Rob muttered.

"They were like undead ants at a picnic," Jools said. "Looks like the trees have grown back, though."

The downhill ride took them swiftly from the hot heights and through a temperate zone at the edge of the ice plains. Rob felt the temperature drop with every step Saber took. Before them, a long-ago snowfall had left the odd spruce and oak trees draped in lacey flakes that hadn't melted. The sky was a silvery blue, dotted with ice-cube clouds. Cold, packed snow squeaked beneath the horses' hooves.

Suddenly, Jools and Beckett stopped. Jools held up a hand and listened. "What's that?"

Rob heard a far-off whining that rose and fell, like some sort of power tool from his old world. "It's coming from the direction of the village."

The riders urged their horses along the empty minecart tracks until they spied the icy towers of Spike City, the largest settlement Rob had encountered in the southern hemisphere. He remembered it as a harsh, yet beautiful place. They drew closer, and the whining got louder. The riders could see movement on the outskirts of town.

Beckett's potion had worn off and Saber's instincts had kicked in. Both horses slowed to a crawl, not wanting to approach the strange noise. When they got near enough to see shiny objects whirling through space, it was all Rob and Jools could to do to press them forward.

Finally, the animals stopped altogether, tense as two creepers ready to explode. Rob couldn't believe his eyes.

The minecart tracks ended abruptly. Someone had scavenged them and laid out an oval track outside the city walls. Around and around on the rails flew several souped-up minecarts, piloted by players in black leather jackets and round mirrored sunglasses. There was much pumping of fists and yelling in a language Rob couldn't distinguish.

One of the drivers noticed the upset horses and decided to "help" by blasting a bullhorn of some kind as his cart passed by. Saber kicked out at the new threat. Beckett recapped his bee-sting act, nearly unseating Jools before he could be brought under control. The other drivers jeered loudly, continuing their circuit. Rob thought it best to dismount and lead the horses into the city. Jools gladly agreed.

They made their way to the village gate, where a snow golem was tethered. The guard paid them no mind. The horses followed Rob and Jools down the main street of town, which was neatly paved with packed ice. Greens and colorful vegetables spilled from a covered garden near the town well. Large ice spikes of various dimensions lined the path, and every now and then a resident or worker would enter or exit one of the hollowed-out structures. Rob noticed that many of the buildings had been renovated since he'd last been to the city, sporting a new front porch or covered flowerboxes. Even the passersby appeared more flush, in their crisp aprons and tidily patched robes.

"Here's the church," Rob said, relieved that Frida's low-life brother, Rafe, no longer presided over the congregation. He had been defrocked and replaced with a more reputable cleric. Through the efforts of Judge Tome, the new church director had agreed to act as biome delegate and urged the citizenry to embrace unification.

A plump woman answered the bell and embraced them like long-lost friends. She wore a flowing, wine-colored robe and a garland of roses in her long, thick black hair. "I am Gaia," she said.

Rob introduced himself and Jools, and mentioned that they were on UBO business.

"Delightful," she said. "Come in, come in! Bring your horses."

The priest ushered them into the packed-ice chapel—a dazzling space with sparkly walls, an arched ceiling, and lovely stained-glass windows. Benches filled only half of the vast space, so the horses were parked near a pillar and the troopers invited to a cozy conversation pit carved into the ice. They settled down on some cushions set around a decorative lava lamp.

Gaia brought an armload of hay for Beckett and Saber, and some sweetened elixir for the men to drink while they discussed government matters. Jools delivered the official papers. Rob asked about the cleric's background.

"I come from an order dedicated to the poor," Gaia began. "Unlike the previous pastor here, who dedicated himself to easy money."

Rob nodded. "Old Rafe turned out to be a cleric without a soul."

Jools stroked his chin. "I wondered what happened after Frida gave him a taste of his own medicine."

Gaia replied, "Conscience prevailed. Folks got tired of black market dealings and wanted to improve Spike City's image."

The village outpost had been known to attract the fringe element—griefers, con men, and desperate people who'd fled more lawful or more dangerous environments. These groups often clashed, and there was no police force to quell them. When the citizenry ousted Rafe and looked for a more legitimate replacement, Gaia had stepped in to help them find their moral compass.

"We've made progress in restoring order," the cleric said proudly. "Prosperity helps. Without the syndicate siphoning off resources, folks have more means and less incentive to pilfer."

"What about that welcoming party we saw on our way in?" Rob asked.

Gaia glanced in the direction of the minecart gang. "We still have a ways to go," she admitted. "Our few hired security guards aren't enough. The Thunder Boys moved in awhile back, looking to take advantage."

Jools murmured, "Thunder Boys, Thunder Boys . . . Wait. I know them! One of the *bōsōzoku* gangs. That means *crazy, out-of-control speed freaks.* Basically scoff-laws on wheels."

Rob's eyes widened. "Are they dangerous?"

"More like, unpredictable."

"How so?"

"I hear they enjoy thrashing innocents with wooden swords and lobbing flaming debris through windows. Generally making a pig's ear of things, just for kicks."

"But they're really only kids," Gaia said, defending them. "Kids who have lost their way."

"Sounds like they can still cause a lot of damage. We won't be able to send in peace officers for some time." Rob worried that one of their two supporting villages would pose a bigger threat than they could handle from afar. "In this unification phase, ma'am, we need . . . predictable allies. How do you propose we handle these guys?"

"Simple." Gaia's eyes twinkled. "Employ them."

*

Like a wolf with a fresh skeleton bone, Jools seized on Gaia's idea for taming the youth gang, and he wouldn't let go. Put to constructive use guarding the new UBO transit system, the Thunder Boys could satisfy their wanderlust and stay out of trouble at the same time. As Gaia had said, prosperity could be a great motivator. Even Rob had to admit that he'd rather channel their energy than be victimized by it.

Jools checked the church's computer network connection, and the cleric offered to fetch the minecart gang for an introduction.

"We have to get back to camp," Rob apologized. "But they're welcome to come to Beta for interviews. Would you tell them? There'd be room and board and pay in exchange for their . . . expertise."

"I'm grateful for you being open-minded," she said. "And for your part in bringing the Overworld back together. Life in the southern hemisphere has been trying since the breakup."

She rose and went to a side table and returned with a glass vessel. It contained an unusual green liquid that Rob had never seen before.

Jools knew its value, though. "A bottle o' enchanting! Where'd you get that?"

"For you. In gratitude," the priest said.

"Just what I need! I've died so many times and enchanted so many things that I have a devil of a time collecting XP."

Rob looked from Turner to Gaia. "XP?"

"Experience points. Needed for weapons and armor enchantment," Gaia explained.

At Rob's blank stare, Jools reached for the gift and said, "Don't worry about that. Leave the enchanting to me." He turned the bottle this way and that. "It's so pretty, I think I'll set it on the mantle in my bunk for a bit before breaking it."

Huh? Rob didn't want to appear more ignorant, so he didn't ask how the thing worked. He assigned potion brewing to Jools, who was always happy to share his concoctions. Surely the battalion would benefit from his added XP and enchantment powers.

The cavalry commander preferred to get his experience in person, anyway. He thanked Gaia for her hospitality and collected the horses. Then he and Jools headed back to Beta to assess the building progress, exiting through the village's far gate to avoid worrying the horses.

"Guess we'll have to get Beckett and Saber 'Thunder Boys' broke," Rob said to Jools, "if we do hire them."

"Oh, we must!"

The quartermaster babbled on about railway matters as the horses picked their way to the summit and down the northern slope of the extreme hills. "I'm keen to see what the colonel and judge have to say about our new transit blokes," he said.

Rob's concern for those they'd left behind drifted over him. "I hope everything is okay with the city. Can't wait to get back," he said, without confiding his reasons. Ever since Fate had removed him from his home environment, he'd enjoyed returning from travels to whatever temporary base camp they'd staked out. He needed that moment of recognition and comfort now to put his niggling doubts about the Beta project to rest.

But rest did not await him.

The riders meant to put the horses up in cavalry camp first, but a disturbance at the village gate caught their attention as they rode by. A noisy crowd of people had gathered, and the twin iron golems could barely hold them back. Rob noticed that many of those gathered waved flyers and carried sacks stuffed with inventory.

He eyed Jools. "You don't suppose . . ."

". . . your advert! Appears to have done its job," Jools said.

"And then some. You think all of these folks are pioneers?" Rob asked weakly. "There must be a hundred of them! But . . . we're nowhere near ready for moving day." The reality of having more souls to shelter overwhelmed the captain, who—up until now—had found it difficult to keep a mere handful of cavalry soldiers in line.

They rode toward the gate, and the crowd parted to let Saber and Beckett clop past.

"Take a number!" Stormie's forceful shout sailed over the clamor. "Everyone'll get a turn. Now, ma'am—"

"Artilleryman!" Rob hailed Stormie, who was attempting to pacify a large, red-faced woman while handing out tickets to the crowd and peeling the grimy fingers of three small, yelping children from her ankles.

She jerked her head up impatiently, then smiled when she noticed Rob and Jools. "Am I ever glad to see y'all," she said, dislodging the ankle-biters, who promptly began to cry at the top of their lungs. "We've got a situation."

"I can see that," Rob said, trying to keep a straight face as amusement broke through his worry.

The children noticed the horses and set upon them. One shoved a handful of prickly cactus needles in Saber's face, yelling, "Eat! Eat!" The other two attempted to climb up Beckett's tail.

"For the love of mods," Jools said to Stormie, "open the gate and let us in!"

She did as he asked, narrowly averting a stampede by yanking the chainmail barrier shut behind them.

Then, she turned her back on the unruly throng, leaned backward, and slid slowly down the gate to the ground.

Rob and Jools dismounted and stared through the mesh fence at the pandemonium on the other side. "What in the Overworld is going on?" Rob asked.

Stormie rubbed her temples. "It's a long story, sir."

"Give me the short version."

She told him that soon after he, Jools, and Kim had left for the plains, people had begun arriving. Some wanted to deliver their residency applications in person, some wanted jobs, and some folks had simply packed up all their belongings and shown up, ready to move in.

"It would seem that support for biome unification is more widespread than we thought," Jools observed.

"It's true," Stormie said. "We're too popular. Frida's been interviewing prospects for two days straight."

Rob groaned. "This is one problem we didn't think of in advance." He cast another glance at the restless mob. "How're we gonna feed all these people?"

"Well, Captain, we can either feed 'em or let 'em become fodder for the mobs tonight."

For an instant, Rob actually considered the latter solution. But Jools had already put his mind to work.

"Leave it to me," said the quartermaster. "I've got the keys to the pantry. Besides, with a little food for bait, I'll have all our manpower issues solved in a tick."

"Right, team," Rob said. "Let's catch up with the others and get them on board ASAP."

The crowd outside started to chant: "Let—us—in! Let—us—in!"

Rob faced them, waving his arms, and raised his voice. "You, people! Just be patient, and we'll find food and shelter for everyone."

This only agitated them. Some began rattling iron ingots against the chainmail gate. "Let—us—in! *Let—us—in!*"

Rob turned to Stormie with apprehension. "Looks like their patience is shot. Is Kim back yet?"

Stormie motioned in the direction of the modest stone building they were using as a city hall until the capitol campus was done. "Everybody's in there." She turned to Jools. "You'd better come up with lunch fast, bro, if you want to avoid a riot."

*

They left the iron golems to deal with the crowd and found Judge Tome, Colonel M, and Kim helping Frida with her paperwork at a table in the conference room. When Rob asked, Kim reported that Swale and the ponies were doing fine. Rob sent Stormie for De Vries and Crash.

"Any news from our delegates?" Judge Tome inquired Rob while the group waited.

"They're up to speed and ready for action. We've got Aswan checking the grapevine for any griefer activity directed at us. Gaia is providing some . . . qualified staff for Jools's transit venture. There's still some unrest in Spike City, but she's of the mind that steady work will pacify any yahoos or malcontents."

"A wise move," Colonel M said. "Precisely what I would have done."

Jools filled in what he knew about the renegade minecart gang and described his plan to transform them into law-abiding transit police. They could double as a railway building and maintenance crew. "Given the present situation, we should fast-track that development." He saw Kim wince and added, "Pun intended."

"How's the application screening going?" Rob asked Frida.

The vanguard was living up to her position as scout. "I've rejected some known griefers that were in our system, and I'm about halfway through the stack," she said, pointing to the documents that had accumulated. "Since we've got folks here asking for work, I started personal interviews so we can hire new hands right away. Maybe step up the pace of construction."

"Good. I imagine we'll be able to move up our ribbon-cutting date."

Stormie arrived with the brother-and-sister building team, and Rob asked them for an update on the project status.

De Vries strode over to a 3-D model of the proposed city that covered one end of the long table. He pushed his sandy hair out of his eyes and pointed at various wooden blocks. "We're in this building here, next to the site HQ. We've laid a foundation for the capitol's legislative chambers and administrative offices—here and here. The well has been dug and a patch for the veggie farm leveled, over this way. I'm assuming you've brought the first items for planting."

Jools nodded, now especially grateful for the seedlings Swale had given them to carry back. "More to the point, De Vries, old chap, what about the residences?"

The architect frowned. "We only expected a few dozen immigrants at first, and certainly not so soon. Nothing's ready."

"Well, what have you designed?" Rob asked.

De Vries gestured to a couple of cul de sacs off the main street of the model, where single-family dwellings were to be built.

Rob pictured the raucous scene at the gate again. "That won't cut it. What we need are apartments. *Now.*"

Crash got up and pointed to an adjacent area on the model, and then drew three imaginary towers in the air with her pickaxe.

"High rises!" Jools interpreted. "Wicked smart. But how long will that take?"

Crash raised her eyes to the ceiling.

Jools slapped his palms on the table. "We're on the verge of mutiny. We've got to increase the workforce straight away. Meanwhile, we'll need to take some emergency measures to mollify the masses."

Stormie raised a pinky finger. "And step up defense, pronto. Otherwise, those good people are gonna be some monster's midnight snack."

Rob's head spun with the number of pressing tasks that all needed to be addressed at once. "We'll talk security in a minute. First, we've got to come up with a way to get those pilgrims off the city's doorstep. We can't have villagers living in a construction site." He glanced at Colonel M. The old ghost probably had the most experience in dealing with large groups. "Any ideas, sir?"

The colonel gave a judicious nod in Jools's direction. "Your quartermaster is adept at detail management. I suggest he begins delegating." The sound of shouting settlers rose in the distance. "And quickly."

CHAPTER 5

THE ADMINISTRATIVE COMMITTEE DECIDED THAT an emergency shelter adjoining the cavalry camp should be raised right away. It was the only piece of ground near Beta that was large and flat enough to accommodate so many people. Housing the homeless in tents there would allow Battalion Zero to defend them from hostiles at night . . . and police any unsavories who might cause trouble. Rob ordered Stormie to get a head count and De Vries and Crash to work on the tent city immediately.

Jools continued delegating. With Stormie's help, Frida would document and process the incoming residents, issuing each able body a job in camp or construction. "Kim, you'll take a crew to harvest those huge mushrooms we saw in the underground circular cave. Mushroom stew will extend the most in feeding folks until we get that garden up and running. If we craft enough bone meal for fertilizer, we could be picking veggies within a few days. As far as importing farm animals and other resources, the minecart system should enable adequate transport soon. I'll get right on it."

"Excellent, Quartermaster." Rob felt himself relax slightly, now that the gargantuan undertaking had been broken down into simpler parts.

"That just leaves defense," Judge Tome reminded him. "We'll still need to safeguard the miners and builders, as well as the new residents."

"We're stretched thin as it is," Rob said. "I'll get Turner to recruit volunteers for a night guard." He stood up. In the confusion he had overlooked the sergeant's absence. "Has anyone seen Turner?"

Nobody had.

Frida suggested checking in on the new hires— Turner had said something about getting up a card game with them. She, Kim, and Jools took off to go help Stormie move the settlers downhill to cav camp and get them organized. Rob walked over to the trailer that housed the job offices, to look for Turner.

As his foot touched the porch steps, he smelled smoke and heard laughter coming from within. He threw the door open without knocking and entered, surveying the scene. A plank had been laid on a block to fashion a card table, and several players sat around it, engrossed in a game. Rob recognized only Turner, who had a tall stack of wooden chips before him and an attractive woman seated at his side. A redstone aroma diffuser filled the air with smoke-scented fragrance.

Turner, his back to Rob, took off his yellow miner's cap and plunked it on the woman's head. She giggled. He addressed the men: "So, finally, the fella walks into the butcher shop and says, 'Two cow patties—hold the cow!' Ya get it?" He waited for laughs, but the others had noticed the captain and gone silent. "I know *you* get it, Rose." Turner tickled the woman, and she giggled again.

Then his eyes slowly followed the gaze of the players at the table. He turned around to see the captain regarding him with displeasure.

Anger shot through Rob as though his body were a creeper's short fuse. "Sergeant?"

Turner fumbled for words. "W-we was just . . ."

"I can see what you 'was just' doing. Slacking off while on duty." Rob shook his head grimly. "Sergeant, are you taking money from these men? Aren't you supposed to be screening them for employment? And who, may I ask, is this woman?"

Turner stared at his commander dumbly for a moment. Then excuses spilled out of him: "My pay's been frozen, if you'll recollect. And I *am* doin' my job.

These here folks're interested in gainful work. A fella can learn a lot about a man's character by playin' cards with him."

Rob raised a cowboy boot and sent it crashing against the tabletop, upsetting the cards and shooting chips into the air. They rained onto the floor like hail. "Game over!" he shouted. "Sergeant, get these people down to cavalry camp with the rest of the settlers." Rob regained his manners, and turned to address the woman. "Begging your pardon, ma'am."

She gave a watered-down giggle, which trickled away to nothing.

Turner reached over and retrieved his cap, jamming it on his head backwards. The redstone lamp shone in Rob's face, making him flinch.

"Cap'n," Turner said over his shoulder, in a conciliatory voice, "let me introduce you two." He slung an arm around the woman's neck. "This here's Rose."

"Rose?" an incredulous Rob repeated. "This is no time for socializing."

Turner let go of the woman and got up to face him. "We ain't. At least, that ain't all we're doin'. I'ma get her a job." Seeing Rob's skeptical look, he explained, "She's an interior decorator. Loads of experience. Which we're bound to need. What with all these buildings and stuff."

Rose turned dramatically toward the captain, her pleading eyes and clasped hands enhanced by

oversized, modified purple eyelashes and fingernails.
"I want to do my part. The UBO should have a well-appointed capitol building. Turnie says you're hiring."
She exchanged an intimate smile with the sergeant,
then sent one in Rob's direction.

"Well, I—could put in a word for you with De
Vries. He's the lead architect. It'd be his decision."

Rose pooched out her purple-varnished lips at
him. "Pretty please."

Rob colored. "Well, I . . . I'll see what I can do.
Sergeant, we need a security detail. Top priority. Enlist
these men as military police," he ordered Turner. Then
he waved at the game board and chips that littered the
floor. "And clean this mess up!"

*

The more work he gave the mercenary to do, Rob
had noticed, the less opportunity Turner had to cause
trouble. Rob stepped outside the trailer and made his
way to the main gate, where the crowd had begun to
disperse. He slipped through and joined the exodus
headed for cavalry camp.

Never a dull moment, he thought, actually longing
for a string of dull moments. But night was coming
on, and it wouldn't do to have dozens of unprotected
citizens milling about as mob bait. The battalion
needed to get the immigrants fed and sheltered, and

signed up for work detail. *Idle hands make the Nether's work*, he reminded himself.

Rob was pleased to see that Quartermaster Jools had already divided the crowd into manageable groups. Some gathered around Kim to receive housekeeping and foraging duties, while a team directed by Crash erected large bunk tents. Many were still complaining loudly and demanding something to eat. Rob hoped the activity would calm them down. He approached Frida and De Vries, who were busy processing a line of experienced workers being considered for Beta project employment.

"How goes it, De Vries?"

The architect motioned one of the chosen applicants over to a pile of protective suits and caps and then gave Rob a big grin. "Toppie! Couldn't have asked for a better boost to our crew. This will cut build time in half."

Frida spoke up. "In a way, it's good we were forced to hire on more people. De Vries always wants to do it all himself."

"Well, when you're the best . . ." the builder said.

Someone pushed through the line, causing grumbling among those waiting their turn.

Rob heard a familiar persuasive voice: "Move aside, coming through."

"Ow!" said one worker in line as Rose dug her fingernails into his shoulder and marched past.

She linked arms with Rob so he couldn't escape. "Did you tell him?" she demanded. "Did I get the job?" She fixed her eyes on him like he was the only man in the Overworld.

Rob was both attracted and repulsed, but found himself unable to look away. Frida and De Vries stared at Rose, and then at Rob.

"This is . . . Rose," the captive captain mumbled. "She's come in search of work—"

She dropped a sheet of scented stationery on Frida's folding table. "My résumé." Releasing and immediately ignoring Rob, she turned her attention to the vanguard.

Frida sized her up, then quickly scanned the sheet of paper. "Interior designer, you say." She swept the paper into a rubbish container. "Nonessential. Sorry. Our man De Vries does all his own interior work. Kind of a control freak that way."

Rose turned the full force of her enhanced beauty on the building engineer, bowling him over. Without saying a word, she reduced the normally steadfast man to the consistency of a slime block.

De Vries gave Frida a shaky glance. "Now, let's not be hasty," he said, moving around to the front of the table and taking Rose by the elbow. "Why don't you tell me more about your experience . . . ?"

"No need fer that," came a hurried interjection from Turner, who was hustling up to the pair. "Lady's already showed me her . . . portfolio." He gave De Vries an absent pat on the back and ushered Rose away. "I'll vouch for her."

Frida frowned. "I'm not so sure *I* will. . . ."

The next fellow in line stepped up and leaned his elbows on the table, interrupting.

"Can I help you?"

A player with olive-green skin coloring, similar to Frida's, and long, thick, curly dark hair perched there. A guitar hung casually from a strap over one shoulder. "It's me can help you," he said in a voice that was rich and deep and promising. "That is, *I*. It is I who has come—no, *have* come—to offer my services in a way that could be most assist-ful."

The others stopped what they were doing. Rose shifted her attention to the young gentleman.

"What I mean to say is, I can help." He pushed back his locks and shook even more volume into them.

Frida regarded him with awe. "How . . . so?"

"Allow me to play you a song. A ditty. A lullaby. A soothing tune," the man said, reaching for his guitar.

Frida swooned as the musician favored them with a sweet, sultry ballad. When he finished, she sat there, mesmerized.

"Bra-*vo*!" said Rose, clapping appreciatively until Turner shushed her.

Frida remained captivated.

Rob narrowed his eyes. He had never seen the normally outspoken vanguard tongue tied. "We've no call for *musicians*," Rob said, as though turning away a snake-oil salesman.

"Oh, I think you do, friend. I saw how you handled those people at the gate. It wasn't exactly effective. Fruitful. Productive. That is to say: it didn't work."

Rob needed no reminder of that. "It's *captain*. And I'm not your friend."

The man grinned. "I will be, once I've sung them all to sleep." He cocked his head at the camp full of tired, hungry people.

Frida snapped out of it and shuffled some papers on the table. "We . . . might be able to find a place for you. What did you say your name was?"

The man offered her a card. "Gratiano, at your service. Your wish is my command. I'm your man—"

Rob reached out and snatched the card. Frida leaned over to read along with him:

GRATIANO782
Guitarist
Weddings – Parties – Bar Mitzvahs

The captain caught Frida's gaze and shook his head ever so slightly.

She shot him an *I've got this* look and took the card from him. She smiled at Gratiano. "Of course, the

UBO capital city will welcome the arts. There'll be state functions, parades, and the like. Meanwhile, you can help keep the peace in camp." She held a hand out for him to shake.

He took it and kissed it. "My"—he searched for the right word, or string of words—"pleasure."

*

Gratiano played more tunes, serenading workers as they went about their tasks. To Rob's annoyance, his singing did seem to improve the settlers' moods.

At Crash's command, her crews placed stacks of wooden fencing in squares as tent walls, and spread wool and planks overhead to roof the structures. Dozens of residents were issued shovels and put to work hollowing out a rough ditch around the camp. This wouldn't prevent mobsters from getting at the inhabitants, but it would give the guards an advantage in picking enemies off. Jools had vetoed using Beta's power tools or anything else of value from the project's inventory stores, but the number of helpers—and a willing attitude—made the work go quickly.

The emergency shelters were soon up, and the aroma of mushroom stew hung in the air as the sun sank.

"You, men! Over here!" called Turner. Rob had forcibly removed his sergeant from Rose's side and ordered him to assemble a protective detail. Turner had armed his poker buddies with wooden swords and axes, and instructed them to fan out along the trench.

Jools asked the cavalry to perform double duty that evening. They could play decoy, luring skeletons that spawned away from camp. Then they could hunt them down and kill them for their bones. "We need as much bone meal as we can craft for the village garden," he reminded Rob over dinner. "That way, all we have to do is irrigate, and we'll be able to start supplying families with food."

Although the troopers were overworked and weary, the prospect of an armed fight energized them. It was, after all, why they had joined ranks in the first place. Rob eagerly awaited sunset.

Turner left the card sharks to guard the camp while he and the rest of Battalion Zero met up in the horse pasture to ready for battle. As Rob saddled Saber, the prospect of danger made him think again of his directive to synchronize spawn points. So far, the only one who would return to safeguard the people and horses after an untimely death was Kim. Rob couldn't leave her—or Saber—in the lurch. *I've got to stay alive long enough to die safely*, he thought, vowing to climb into bed the very next night.

Jools opened the weapons inventory and moved down the line of battalion members, handing out bows and arrows. What a luxury it was to be arming for a hunt instead of a griefer-led onslaught. Rob had never thought he'd look forward to an evening with creepers and skeletons, but now he considered it a chance for some pleasant target practice. He had become pretty good with a bow—at least, compared to the first time he'd picked one up, in the heat of a melee.

Dusk fell. The battalion mounted up and rode out of the pasture in file, via the drawbridge that Frida and Stormie had crafted. At Rob's command, the band rode to the edge of the civilian camp and jumped the small ditch surrounding it—even Jools was able to cross the trench on Beckett.

Rob praised Jools for working on his jumping. "And—what was it? '*Ursula majesty optimum*'—" The captain mangled the Latin. "Practice makes perfect, like the judge says."

*

The sky became inky, splotched by moonlight and spattered with stars. Night sounds rose and fell as unseen hostiles spawned and approached the encampment or changed course. Battalion Zero rode forward to a grouping of rocks outlined on the hillside, beyond which the terrain dipped steeply.

"Front into line, march!" the captain ordered. "…and halt." The six horses stood shoulder-to-shoulder, facing the edge of the clearing, waiting for the mobs to show themselves. "No sense fighting on that slope."

"Let them come to us," Turner agreed.

Suddenly, an explosion rang out, farther down the hill; then another.

"Creepers!" Stormie exclaimed. "Anybody gets a chance, take 'em for their gunpowder. Colonel M wants me to start beefing up the armory. Just think, y'all—Beta will have its own standing army before long, and we'll be free to travel."

"We'll be out of a job, you mean," Turner grumbled.

"This choice position?" Jools said sarcastically. "I get no time off, no health insurance, and no pay— at the moment, anyway. . . ." He trailed off, having touched on a sore subject.

"You all know what you have to do to earn your wages," Rob said stiffly.

"Captain!" Frida called from Ocelot's post, off his left shoulder. "Zombies over that way."

"Let 'em pass. Turner's men are equipped for hand-to-hand combat."

The sergeant tilted his head. "*Turner's men.* Has a nice ring to it—"

Just then, an arrow stuck in his shoulder.

"Son of a—" He pulled the arrow out, leaving an extra rip in his shirt, from which blood oozed.

"*Skellies!*" Jools yelled, raising his bow.

"Fire at will!" Rob called.

A platoon of jittering assailants came at them over the rocks. They were armored with an assortment of somebody's old inventory. Rob cursed his oversight. Without Lady Craven's threat, he'd let his guard down—none of the troopers had bothered with armor tonight.

Then my aim had better be right on, Rob thought, fitting an arrow to the short, reinforced bow that Turner had showed him how to craft. *Th-ang! Ter-wang!* Two shots skipped off of a skeleton's chestplate. The third met bone with a deadened *crunch*.

"Captain!" Kim got his attention. "That rise!"

In the moonlight, Rob saw the slight incline she pointed to. Shooting from it would provide an advantage against their opponents' ragtag armor. "Battalion, right wheel! March!"

They gained ground and turned to face the oncoming phalanx of skeletons.

"Fire!"

Th-th-thoop! Thoop! Thoop! Arrows showered in both directions. Rob's riders knew they had to protect their mounts as well as themselves. They might not have been stronger than the skeletons, but they shot with greater fury and accuracy, giving more hits than they received.

When the last skeleton had ben reduced to a pile of bones, the members of Battalion Zero were damaged, but still standing. Frida and Jools jumped down from Ocelot and Beckett and scooped up the bones and arrows left scattered on the ground. When the battalion remounted, they all rode off toward the other end of camp to patrol the perimeter.

Four more melees yielded full stacks of bones—as many as they could carry. It had been a long, but successful, night. Healing potion and the remnants of mushroom stew awaited the tired troopers. The battalion had retreated toward the civilian zone when another mob of skeletons materialized a few blocks away.

"Have at them!" Jools cried, and motioned for the others to draw their bows.

Through the skeleton ranks, Rob made out a trio of greenish creatures coming their way. *More zombies?* The combatants hesitated, waiting to see what would happen.

P-oom! Th-wang! POOM!

The smoke cleared and dawn light eliminated the remaining mobsters. Then what they'd heard became evident: an exploding creeper had blown up a skeleton, just as it shot another creeper.

"It doesn't get any better than this!" Turner said, swinging out of Duff's saddle to fetch the gunpowder and bones. "Wait! It does!" He held up a skeleton skull and a music disc. "Party in my bunk!"

*

The following day, the residents widened the ditch surrounding civilian camp and increased their night guard so the battalion could get some rest. Once again, Rob had every intention of climbing into his bed, counting sheep, and waking up with a new spawn point. He turned in along with the others and went to his quarters.

As the captain took off his vest and boots, though, he caught himself humming the little tune that he used to sing to Jip, his dog, before tucking him in beside the campfire at night. Then Rob thought of Pistol, his favorite horse back on the ranch. He felt homesick—and that made him mad at himself. His determination wavered. The truth was, as long as he preserved his claim on the original place that had spawned him into this world, there was still a chance he could reverse the process.

Yeah, a chance as slim as my shadow. But Kim had done it—revised her spawn point. And she probably wanted to respawn at her horse farm. Of course, half of her horses were here, now, not a world away on a ranch she might never see again.

The argument ended with Rob stretching out on his bedroll on the floor, thinking, *Just one more night.*

CHAPTER 6

ROB WOKE FROM A TROUBLED SLEEP, WISHING he could go back in time. He got up and fussed around camp, polishing already gleaming swords and grooming a spotless Saber, who didn't mind the extra attention. Meanwhile, his troops were sorting out the Beta details nicely.

Kim designated a farming crew to plant Swale's crops and irrigate and fertilize the new garden. Stormie pried Turner away from Rose and got him to help arm and train another rotation of camp guards, while Jools and Frida got the new hires started working with Crash on the city's residence construction. Rob was glad to have employed all of his troopers, so they wouldn't be . . . distracted by certain new residents. He wandered up to Beta to find something else to do.

He was chatting with Judge Tome and Colonel M when Jools found the group and told them to expect six loud, weird-looking drivers in modified minecarts at the city gates anytime. Word had come from Gaia that she'd talked the Thunder Boys into throwing over their outlaw ways to test-drive a legit job on the rail system.

The quartermaster approached Rob. "I'll take my paycheck now."

For a moment, the captain wondered if he'd offered Jools a bonus for headhunting and forgotten about it. Then he realized what the request meant.

"Well that's—just swell," Rob stammered. He went on, blustering, "I'll hold you up as an example to the other troopers. It's this sort of solidarity that'll ensure our victory, and maybe even make the Overworld a better place."

Jools stood up straighter and tugged on the cuffs of his tweed jacket. "I suppose I am exemplary, now that you mention it. But then, you know what that's like. Right, Captain? How would the others ever get by without us?"

Rob's vision clouded.

"Come to think of it, how would *we* get by without us? I realized the other night that if I died at the hands of some skelemob, I might end up lost in the Nether, and then I'd never get to finish my transit project." He grinned. "It's near and dear to my heart."

"What about the battalion?"

"Oh, yeah. You mates are loves, too." Jools pulled out his computer and went back to working on his drawings for the track layout and station design.

Rob had Jools's pay added to his personal inventory, making sure the other troopers were on hand in camp that afternoon to witness the exchange.

"Y'know, boss," said Turner, "you could give my earnin's to Rose to . . . hold for me. Until such time as you might relinquish 'em, that is."

"You mean, you haven't changed your spawn point?"

Turner grunted.

"It's not so bad, Meat," Jools said, flashing his inventory.

Turner scowled, but didn't respond.

"Jools is right," Kim said. "C'mon, everybody. Three down, three to go! Right, Bat Zero?"

Rob gave her a guilty nod. Jools counted his stacks of gold ore. Stormie, Frida, and Turner wandered off, suddenly remembering something else they had to do on the other side of camp.

By the next day, Rob had come up with yet another excuse for postponing his own commitment to the group. He secretly watched Kim and Jools throw themselves into their work. They looked happier. They had also, he realized, received things they wanted once they'd made the leap: a new foal for Kim, a new project for Jools—not to mention the gold ore they had coming to them. It was as though the universe had rewarded them for following orders. *Was that possible?* Suppose Rob changed his own spawn point and enjoyed some sort of good fortune that he hadn't foreseen. Maybe something even better than going home to his ranch. What would he wish for?

Just then, Rob saw Frida cross the compound with Gratiano. *Well . . . I guess that ain't gonna happen.*

He had never really expressed his feelings for Frida *to* Frida. Getting involved with a fellow trooper could be risky. Besides, it wasn't captain-ly. And even if it were, it seemed that—now—he was too late.

*

A few days later, Rob stood at the edge of civilian camp after dawn and surveyed the scene. The castaway cowboy had never lived in a center of such high activity. All around him was movement: workers filed by with pushcarts full of mushrooms or cobblestone. Foremen squared off in twos and threes to discuss logistics. Pioneer children ran around inside a fenced play enclosure, safely removed from the booby-trapped pasture moat. On the other side of the pit trap the battalion's horses grazed happily.

Kim caught sight of the idle captain and waved him over. "Come to town with me. We're going to start picking the first crops in the garden!" The bone meal fertilizer had done its job. Night torches and redstone lamps placed along the field's edges had allowed fruits and vegetables to grow around the clock.

Rob would've preferred a nice juicy, rare steak, but any variety would do. "I'm sick of mushroom stew," he confided, falling into step with the horse master.

"I'm a little tired of farming and babysitting," Kim admitted. "I'd much rather be picking out hooves and currying coats. It'll be great to get these folks self-sufficient and go back to our own work."

"That's for sure." Feeling he'd lost his chance with Frida, Rob had refocused on his command. "I'd rather play defense than referee. I feel like a glorified house-keeper." He picked up a shovel left on the ground by some resident and leaned it against a fence post.

Rob and Kim approached the chainmail-draped construction site and donned yellow leather caps at the entrance. Crash insisted on head protection, especially now that there was more activity from less-experienced crew members.

WHUMP! Rob jumped. A bucket of heavy pistons clattered to the ground from an overhead scaffold as if to prove the need for Crash's safety measures.

"Swale suggested we pick one quadrant at a time, letting the rest of the crops grow until they're needed," Kim said as they walked toward the center of Beta. "Today, it's melons. We'll be spitting out seeds by nightfall."

Rob could practically taste the sweet fruit. But as he and Kim approached the garden, a settler woman ran toward them waving her arms.

"Captain! Corporal! It's the irrigation. Something's gone bad-wrong!"

Rob and Kim looked at each other, and then ran, following the woman back toward the vegetable patch. An unnatural glow lit the area, and black smoke filled the air.

The farm covered a nine-by-nine–block area of rich soil brought in from the valley delta. De Vries had designed an ingenious canal irrigation system to encircle it, using water from an underground spring and strategically placed flood gates. All the farmers had to do was release the pooled water periodically.

But when the cavalry mates arrived at the garden plot, there was no water—or crops, for that matter—to be seen. Instead, the canals bubbled with reddish-orange lava . . . and only a few blackened stems of the ripening plants floated on top. The bountiful harvest had been reduced to thin wisps of sooty smoke.

Rob and Kim stood as though paralyzed, unable to take their eyes off the grisly sight. De Vries came running, yelling, "I found the source!"

Shaken, the builder described the underground scene he'd discovered. The cavern's spring had been diverted, and a subterranean lava stream was connected to the canal. It had happened sometime between the night watch and dawn. The fledgling garden crops had withered and died when they came in contact with the molten liquid.

"Who could have done this?" Rob asked, voicing everyone's question.

De Vries scowled. "I knew we should never have let unscreened workers on the property."

"Frida did screen them," Rob replied defensively. "Besides, who would've had that kind of underground access?"

"Or the tools or know-how to switch lava for spring water?" Kim added.

De Vries confessed that one of his original crew had been on night watch duty at the excavation sites. The man had been keeping tabs on the hillside's ore deposits and stone quarries, not the farm or its water supply. It seemed unlikely that he would want to sabotage his own job.

A quick survey above ground revealed no evidence of tampering with the gates or canal system, or any break-in through the chainmail fencing. The iron golems were still standing out front, and nothing else seemed amiss.

"We've about exhausted the stock of mushrooms," Kim reminded the captain. "What'll we do?"

Rob pulled off his yellow cap and ran a hand through his flattened hair. "Finding the culprits will have to wait. We'll have to import food—and spend our precious gems. Let's get Jools on it."

Meanwhile, De Vries would have to figure out how to restore fresh water to the canals. "I've never done that before," he admitted, scratching his head. "Bubbling lava has a mind of its own. It doesn't always go where you want it to."

Rob had every confidence that the brilliant engineer would solve the problem, so he and Kim set off to find Jools and tell him the bad news. As they reached the admin offices, however, the quartermaster intercepted them.

"There you are! Quick! The conference room. We've got a call waiting from Aswan. He told me to fetch you, sir, and Turner."

"Turner?"

"Maybe Aswan has some more leather goods for him."

"I'll just head back to the cavern for the last of the mushrooms, then." Kim excused herself.

Turner was handling the blocks on the site model when Jools and Rob entered the room.

"Put those down!" Rob scolded and headed for the computer screen.

Jools clicked on something, and Aswan's face appeared.

"Greetings, Captain!"

"What is it, Delegate?"

Aswan looked over both shoulders, as though someone might be watching him. "I've got intel on the intel," he whispered.

Jools leaned into camera range. "Speak freely, Aswan. This connection's guaranteed secure. Have you got news of griefers trying to undermine our operation?"

The tradesman relaxed. "Well, I started poking around the indie riffraff, asking if anyone had heard about the syndicate or allied griefer army stirring up trouble in the extreme hills. I didn't mention your city construction."

"Well played," Jools murmured.

"A couple of men—low types, to be sure—said they'd heard the syndicate had gone underground but was still doing Lady Craven's bidding. I'll wager their stories stick since I asked them separately and they both told the same tale."

"Classic interrogation technique," Rob said, admiring Aswan's work.

"So, I put out feelers to find the location of either the syndicate's base camp or where Lady Craven and her griefers are holing up."

"Did you get the sense they were even in this game mode?" Jools asked. He wondered if his effort in shifting the griefer queen from Survival to Creative mode had produced lasting consequences.

Aswan shrugged. "Wherever she is, she's still controlling Overworld filth who mean to prevent any unification of the biomes. That much seems clear."

"How so?" asked Rob.

"I managed to intercept a sonic transmission sent to your area. It was scrambled, but all signs point to a Griefer Imperial Army source. No other group would want to face off with a resurrected UBO government."

"Where was it coming from?"

"I couldn't get a send point, but the receiver was definitely in local skip range. Considering the extreme hills summit is the highest point in this hemisphere, it would be the most probable spot to pick up airwave communications that someone didn't want traced."

"Yes, yes. But what did the message *say?*" Jools wanted to know.

"As I mention, it was scrambled. But I did make out the words *plans* and *caverns*. And a name of some sort. It was cut off, but it sounded like *—ermite.* Could it be *endermite?*"

Jools nodded. "Could well be."

"What's an endermite?" Rob asked. He thought he'd encountered every inhabitant of the Overworld. "Are they baby endermen?"

"Hardly," Jools said. "No relation. They're nasty little bugs, like silverfish."

"But harmless?" A mite didn't sound dangerous to Rob.

Aswan shook his head. "They're tiny, but if they get in enough hits, they kill just as big as any other hostile."

"Seems like a strange threat to send our way."

"But one we wouldn't expect," Jools said.

Rob thought this over. "Aswan, keep searching for a send point. And for any news of Lady Craven and her gang. We need to know where they are so we can get between them and these . . . enderboys. Break up their little club."

Jools nodded. "Divide and conquer."

Aswan accepted the task. "I'll see what else I can find out as soon as possible." He made to end the transmission, then asked one more question. "Is Sergeant Turner there? I have someone who wants to speak with him."

Rob motioned for Turner to join the call.

"Hello, my knight in shining armor." A sturdy woman with ruddy skin filled the screen. Her red-dyed hair was pinned up with a couple of horseshoe nails.

"Sundra!" Surprise mixed with guilt in Turner's tone and expression. "I, er, how's it goin', sweets?" Turner flashed an imploring glance at Rob and Jools, as though they might save him. "It's my old lady!" he stage-whispered to them.

"I missed you last time you were in town, hon," the blacksmith said. "Just hope you and the cavalry are safe and well fed."

"Oh, we are that. Fat and happy," Turner lied.

"When are you coming to see me?" Sundra asked.

Turner fidgeted. "Ya know, I'd like to. It's just, I've been—well busy. Real busy lately." He pretended that someone was hailing him off screen. "What's that, General—? Oh, sorry, Sundra. I've gotta go. Duty calls. . . ." He cut her reply short and clicked off. Then he sat back in his chair, obviously perplexed.

"Sundra? I thought *Rose* was your old lady now," Jools needled him.

"Yeah, well. Sundra's my old old lady." Turner got up. "Still carry a torch for her, and all. . . ."

Rob grimaced. "Yeah, a guy can't have too many flames, can he?"

A grin split Jools's face. "Unless they find out about each other."

This brought Turner up short. "Don't you dare—"

"Oh, I would never interfere in another man's relationships," Jools said innocently, stressing the plural. "It's just that, Sundra might need some decorating done on her blacksmith shop. Or Rose might need some specialty armor crafted or a horse shod. You never know."

Turner threw Jools a desperate look, paused, and then dashed out the door.

CHAPTER 7

I F ANY GROUP COULD TURN LEMONS INTO LEMON-
ade, Rob thought, it must be Battalion Zero. In the
past, Frida, Jools, Stormie, Turner, and Kim had
come back from defeat time and again to mount new
attacks on evil. De Vries, Crash, and Judge Tome—
who had been sworn in as privates during the cavalry's
previous campaign—had thrown themselves into the
creation of a new Overworld union. Now the troopers
met each new disaster as though turning bitter fruit
into Kool-Aid.

Jools redoubled his attempts to provide the food
they'd promised the new immigrants. De Vries worked
out the farm irrigation problem. And Frida and Crash
began to poke around for clues as to whoever was trying to disrupt the building of the new UBO capital
city, hoping to avoid another catastrophe.

Action was welcome. The natives were restless.

Once word reached camp about the failed harvest, panic spread among the residents. Rob talked the situation over for an hour with the judge and colonel. He returned to camp to find a settler standing on an upturned box, addressing a knot of disgruntled refugees.

"They say there's nothing left to eat! I say we take what we need from them in charge."

Grumbles ran through the crowd.

The man continued, "They say there's plenty of work. But it ain't worth risking our lives. Today it's lava. What'll it be tomorrow?"

"Spider jockeys!" shouted someone.

"Silverfish!" cried another.

The man on the box raised a fist. "Let's act together. We could just as easily tear this city down as risk our necks building it."

Now Stormie, who had been listening with Jools and Kim nearby, stepped in, jostling the settler off his makeshift stage. "Friends! Don't stir things up before you get the chance at a better life," she counseled.

"But what he said is true!" a settler bellowed.

"Yes." Stormie spread her hands. "The city *is* half-formed. That means it can go either way: down the drain, or toward a stronger, unified biome capital."

This roused some supportive cheers.

"You folks have the power," Stormie conceded. "That's what the United Biomes of the Overworld stands for: power to the people. Now, give us just a little while longer to secure it for you. For everyone!" She glanced over her shoulder at a man who approached her with a request. She nodded and made way for him on the riser.

It was Gratiano, who pulled his guitar from his back and began a folk song—one about the little people overcoming an evil golem.

"Sounds like bloody Gulliver and the Lilliputians," Jools muttered.

"Sounds like he's soothing the savage beasts," Stormie said pointedly, as the upstarts in the crowd settled onto the ground and began swaying and clapping.

Gratiano switched to a love song as Turner strolled up with Rose in tow.

"Why can't you sing to me like that?" she demanded.

"I'm more a fighter than a lover, really," he said. "But I can be romantic." He flexed an arm muscle. "How's *this* for poetry?" A sandstorm appeared to ripple on the desert biome depicted on his biceps.

Now Rob spoke up. "Sergeant, hit the horse corral, on the double. You and Kim will ride out to trade for food from friendlies." Jools had learned that pumpkins could be had from a farmer they knew in the flower forest, and wheat from the fellow Swale had sold his land to when he took over Kim's farm management. "It'll mean a couple days' ride. Whatever you bring back will have to hold us over until the minecart route is completed and we can trade with the villages."

Stormie still looked worried. "What happens between now and then, sir?"

Rob grinned. "Zombie hunt!" Jools had calculated that a sweep for drops could generate enough potatoes and carrots to last a few days.

"Ah, why don't I get to have any of the fun?" Turner groused.

"Kim might need some muscle," Rob reminded him.

"*Rose* might need some muscle," he countered, and then, seeing Rob's stern look, gave up and saluted. "Be back soon," he said, trying to placate his pouting girlfriend.

He left for the horse pasture, and Rose drifted over to listen to Gratiano's performance.

Rob was relieved to have broken up the duo, for now. He remained nearby, keeping an eye on the popular guitarist . . . and the battalion's vanguard.

"What's to be done about the city's burnt-up farm?" Stormie asked him.

"Jools?" Rob said, deferring to the quartermaster.

"When one takes a hit, one rebuilds with a vengeance," he said with determination. "This time, we'll add a second farm level and a waterfall. We can plant the wheat and pumpkin seeds left over from the food trade."

"But, what about the boiling lava?" Stormie demanded.

"That won't happen again," Rob assured her. "De Vries used a redstone wire to send the lava flow downhill. The spring water and canals will get covers to keep the H_2O in and everything else out, plus a permanent guard." He surveyed the crowd warily. "Colonel M says that if we put some of the settlers on watch, they'll have every incentive to keep the resources safe."

Stormie's concerns were not completely eased. "But, sir, how do we guess where lightning'll strike next?"

Rob had already asked himself that question.

"We listen for the thunder."

*

As the three friends spoke, Frida and Crash were seeking out signs of wrongdoing belowground. Thus far, that was where all the trouble had begun. Earlier that day, Rob had appealed to the colonel and judge for their insights. He told them what he'd learned from Aswan and his suspicion that endermites might become a plague.

Colonel M considered this improbable. "I've witnessed the creatures in the Nether, Captain, but not in Overworld caverns."

Judge Tome had argued that slimes would be more likely to spawn or be loosed underground, where the Beta workers were laying foundations or mining for resources. "Although, I don't see how even Lady Craven could enchant slimes to attack the project. There's not much substance to them."

Rob turned other possibilities over in his mind. Whoever—or whatever—had caused the tunnel collapses and irrigation switch could be working alone. He, she, or it might be a player with the syndicate—the loose organization of petty thieves, extortionists, and all-around bad guys looking to gain from others' misfortune. Or the guilty party could be a griefer master of disguise sent by Lady Craven to undo the work of unification. If that were the case, then foiling the crook would involve finding weak links in the job's supply chain.

Rob ordered the vanguard and miner to scout out the next ore pockets planned for use. De Vries had called for crafting hundreds of gold pickaxes in order to gather cobblestone quickly, to satisfy the urgent need for high-rise housing. There was no telling how—or whether—the criminal element was getting inside information on the project, but if it was, then gold mines might be the next target.

Frida and Crash brought Rob news that only heightened the mystery. De Vries joined them in the bunkhouse's common room to discuss what should be done.

"We were too late, Captain," Frida reported darkly.

Crash swung her diamond pickaxe at a half dozen points in the air and then shrugged her shoulders.

"Every documented gold deposit had been mined clean."

This took Rob by surprise. "How?" He turned to De Vries. *"Why?"*

De Vries looked baffled. "Your guess is as good as mine. Whoever did this left veins of diamond and emerald untouched in the same cave system."

"So . . . it's not trade value he's after," Frida surmised.

"Another setback!" Rob muttered. "Now what?"

"A detour," De Vries answered. "We can chop enough wood for the shelters in the oak grove up the hill. We do have plenty of iron axes in our inventory."

"Wooden shelters . . ."

"Not the best material," De Vries admitted. "But it'll do until we're able to upgrade."

"Will we make our deadline?"

The group had revised the date for the city's inauguration. A formal ceremony would feature dignitaries speaking and dedicating the city to Overworld unity. Also, a huge public celebration was planned—but the pioneers would hardly feel like celebrating if their needs were not met.

"I'll move mountains to do it," De Vries vowed. "But what about your end?"

Besides the physical work of constructing the capital city, more biome allies would have to sign on, in order to legitimize a worldwide union.

"We're still working on it," said Frida, who had ridden out with the invitations months ago. They'd received some interest, but still had to finalize terms and select delegates. Rob had planned another outreach mission to the villages in the surrounding jungle, desert, mesa, and plateau biomes, to get firm commitments. However, the construction site and tent city crises had put that important task on hold.

"At least we can point to Sunflower and Spike City as standing with us," Rob said. "Bringing them together with Beta will lay a strong foundation for the UBO. Let's hope it's enough to attract other biomes. When folks see the transit system in place, they'll know we're serious. And Jools tells us that'll be done soon."

A high-pitched whining noise rose in the distance—a sound too unbroken to be part of the chopping or stacking going on in town.

"What the heck is that?" Frida asked.

The noise came closer, growing louder and louder, and more annoying. Then it suddenly stopped.

With a flash of recognition, Rob sensed that Jools's prediction was about to come true.

Everyone who could break away from what they were doing hurried out to where the minecart tracks reached Beta from their precarious summit descent. Turner had once speculated about who had laid the gravity-defying rails up and over the extreme hills. Now the question was, who was crazy enough to ride speeding minecarts on such a trip?

"It's the Thunder Boys," Rob informed Frida and De Vries, who jogged after him to the junction where the tracks split off from Beta toward the sunflower plains.

Stormie, Judge Tome, and Jools met Rob and the others there. Stormie stared in wonder, and the judge nodded in recognition. Jools smiled like an ocelot who'd swallowed a whole chicken.

"They're here!" he cried.

The drivers he and Rob had encountered on the outskirts of Spike City emerged from six custom-ized minecarts. While the young men were dressed identically in black leather jumpsuits and reflective sunglasses, their vehicles each had distinct personal-ities. Colored redstone lights and dye jobs decorated minecarts that had been jacked up, lowered down, or extended until their original designs were barely recognizable. Even the noise they made over typically silent rails was a mod.

Stormie put her hands on her hips. "They sure ain't vanilla."

"I believe I've met those boys in my courtroom a time or two," the judge murmured.

Jools waved the strangers over and attempted to make introductions. The six drivers all began talking at once.

Jools couldn't understand them, and they weren't listening to him. Finally, he asked, exasperated, "But, what are your *names*? I'll need them if you're to get paid."

Again came a flood of speech, none of it intelligible to the quartermaster, who spoke no languages other than his mother tongue.

"All right! Never mind," Jools said. "I'll call you all 'Steve.'"

This seemed to satisfy them, for their sharp chatter dwindled to a buzz.

Frida had come across Gratiano in the gathering crowd, and they approached the welcoming party. "Captain. Gratiano knows what they're saying. He can translate."

"I've spoken that dialect before," Frida's suitor said. "I'll be happy to act as an interpreter. That is, a liaison. Er, a go-between."

Rob blocked the path. He wanted no help from the musician, who might then expect something in return. "I don't think—"

"For gold's sake, Captain. Let him through!" Jools pleaded.

Jools realized an interview would be a waste of time. He instructed Gratiano to get the drivers' signatures on the computer forms that would seal their employment. Then he motioned the minecart gang to the city gate. The musician accompanied them inside to the job office to discuss their duties, obligations, and compensation—and the penalties for any recklessness.

Rob watched them go, feeling a twisting in his gut. "Six more mouths to feed," he said to his remaining troopers. Worse than that, the captain did not feel up to the task of breaking in these new hires—or even watching Jools do so. He made a quick decision.

"Artilleryman," he said, addressing Stormie. "New plan. Frida and I will ride out to the farms with Turner and Kim and do some hunting along the way. No point in buying what we can chase down for free."

"What can I do to help?"

"You can oversee the folks rebuilding the garden. Direct the night guard to cut down some zombies for their drops. Is that clear?"

"Crystal, sir."

Frida touched Rob's shirt sleeve. "Let's get mounted. I can hardly wait to hit the trail."

And he could hardly wait for her to hit it—and get far away from her musical friend. Rob knew that, like himself, the survivalist was more comfortable outside of society than in the thick of it. At least they had that much in common.

CHAPTER 8

ROB WITHDREW SOME GEMS AND ORE INGOTS from what was now the UBO treasury, and the squadron prepared the saddle and pack animals. Food from hunting or trading would be hauled back to camp by the battalion's trusty packhorse, Rat, and not-so-trusty mule, Norma Jean. The small but sturdy buckskin horse and the chocolate-brown mule were each prepared to pull several pack wagons lashed together. They'd find forage en route. The troopers would also have to fend for themselves on the trail. Due to the supply shortage, their personal inventories contained more weapons than rations.

Stormie waved to them as they left camp, with Frida taking the vanguard position on Ocelot and Turner riding Duff behind them. Kim and Rob, mounted on Nightwind and Saber, each led a pack train. Unfortunately, Rob rode downwind of Norma Jean, while little Rat and his carts brought up the rear. It was well after noon when "Operation Chow," as Kim was calling the mission, got underway, leaving only a few hours' daylight in which to ride safely. The squadron would be passing through the cold taiga on its way south, and dusk could fall earlier in the snowy biomes.

"I don't mind riding at night, Captain," Frida said. "We're armed. Might as well keep moving, right? Better to finish this chore sooner than later."

Rob, already treated to the odor of Norma Jean's gas passing, didn't argue. "Let's get it over with," he agreed.

The long ride would bring them closer to the plains, where they'd be trading for wheat. They took their time climbing the extreme hills to preserve the horses' energy. The party followed the minecart tracks up and up. Gravel gradually replaced dirt blocks, and vegetation became scarcer the higher they climbed. Squares of white clouds floated lazily by, reminding Rob of the snowy ground that lay ahead. *What a strange world it is where the sky in one place resembles the earth in another*, he thought.

They stopped to admire the dizzying view at the summit and let the pack animals rest. Plentiful, low-flying clouds limited visibility today, but Rob still counted at least ten biomes, plus the one in which they stood. He dismounted and dropped Saber's reins.

The others got down to stretch. While the animals nuzzled for nonexistent grass, Turner and Kim moved off to enjoy the southern vista. Frida approached the captain.

Rob stared wistfully in the other direction, toward the ocean where he had entered the game. Now that he finally had a chance to observe the landscape, he didn't know what to do about it. A person couldn't see a place in time.

"Thinking of home?" Frida asked quietly.

Rob didn't answer immediately. He kicked at some rocks and made a half circle in the dust with the toe of his boot. "Just . . . thinking," he finally replied. "Seems like I've been here a lifetime already."

"*Lifetime* is relative, sir."

He looked at her from the corner of his eye. "Reckon mine would've been lots shorter, if it weren't for you."

"Reckon mine would've been a lot less interesting, if not for you. Newbie," she added playfully, reminding them both that they'd been friends first, soldiers second.

Now he met her gaze. "No." He paused. "Really?"

"Boundary guarding sure jazzed up my nights, anyway." She smiled.

"Mine, too," Rob admitted. They'd spent many a hectic evening fighting side by side against Lady Craven's enchanted mobs in an effort to stop the griefer queen from claiming biome boundaries. "That's not to say I wouldn't mind some peace and quiet."

"Is it really so different where you come from?" she asked.

"Yes . . . and no." The Overworld was like a fun-house mirror image of his world. How could he explain the totality of existence there? The pace of days and nights, the sense of right and wrong, the *smell* of the place? "It's just . . . I wish I could take you there someday."

Frida walked away a couple of paces. "Well, you know, the jungle's where I belong. Probably wouldn't be much good to you out on the range."

This slammed a picture of home into his brain. "I think you'd love it," he argued, the vision expanding and taking over his senses. "You should see it, Frida. In the West, even when it's dry and dusty underfoot, the sky wants to unfurl forever. And when it gets hot out, nothin' tastes so good as a cold drink from a high-country stream. Best of all, in summer, days don't end till well into the night when the coyotes start singing." Rob thought of Gratiano, who waited for Frida back in town. "Not that you'd be super impressed by that kind of music," he mumbled.

"No," Frida said softly. "It sounds nice."

The others came their way. "Daylight's burnin' up like an old torch," Turner pointed out. "Let's cowboy outta here."

The spell broken, Rob ordered the squadron to collect their horses. Then they pushed on toward the southern hemisphere.

On the descent, Frida called over her shoulder, "This route looks awfully familiar, doesn't it?" They had reached the area where they'd performed a shady job to fund their Overworld defense a while back— escorting the griefer Bluedog's loot.

"At least this time we're on the right side of the law," Rob remarked.

Turner twisted around in his saddle. "Don't know as I like pullin' this job for the white hats 'stead of the black. Makes me feel . . . dirty."

Just then, Norma Jean set to braying. She half-rose in the cart traces and crashed her hooves to earth, once, twice, three times.

"Look out, guys!" Kim dropped the mule's lead rope and drew her sword. "A silverfish!"

The horse master had to wait until Norma Jean paused in her thrashing and the hostile arthropod quit dodging her feet to get a clear shot. As Kim slashed at the tiny wriggling beast, though, her hand slipped, and she barely clipped it. Turner dropped out of his saddle, pulled one of the diamond axes from his dual shoulder holsters, and dispatched it.

"There'll be more!" Frida cried. "Get ready—and make your shots count!" Wounding the mobsters would only spawn more of them.

"Here they come. Dismount to fight on foot!" ordered Rob, hoping the horses would recall their training and wouldn't run off, despite their instincts. Turner pulled his second axe, and the rest of the troopers raised weapons.

It was unnerving, waiting for the silverfish to get close enough to ensure a single clean hit from their blades. Frida especially hated the swarming mobsters for that very reason. Rob recalled that they could be lured out into the sunlight long enough to kill them, but on this steep grade, the pack animals would be goners in a race.

Rob, Frida, Turner, and Kim stood with weapons drawn while countless silverfish homed in on their departed brother's location and tracked the players. Rob felt his skin crawl at the same pace as the eight-legged creatures.

"Get 'em each with one blow!" Turner reminded everyone. "That'll end this."

Rob held his breath as he slashed and missed with his iron sword, wishing it were lighter wood. *A clean miss is okay*, he told himself. *Just remember, kill—don't stun.*

He got the hang of the silverfishes' stop-and-start motion, and found better luck stabbing at them than slashing. When the tide of arthropods at his feet receded, he glanced up and saw that his friends had exterminated their attackers.

"Rob!" yelled Frida. "One more!"

All he saw was a flash before the chittering thing bit him.

"Ow!" Rob stabbed at it so hard that his sword impaled the silverfish and stuck in the rocks.

For a few moments no one moved.

"Is that it?" Frida asked warily.

"Think so," replied Kim, reaching for poor Norma Jean's lead rope.

"Mw-augh," Frida exclaimed with a shudder. "I can't stand silverfish."

"They shouldn't be out here in the bright sun. Where d'you think they came from?" Kim asked.

"They generally hatch out of monster eggs, don't they?" said Rob.

"Yeah, but down under," Turner replied.

As Frida took up Ocelot's reins, she noticed something on the ground. "Hey, what's this?" There sat a small cairn of stones, with an empty spawn egg lying next to it.

"That don't look natural," Turner said.

Kim squatted down for a closer view. "There's no tunnel that the silverfish could've come out of. Somebody put this here!"

"Then, let's get *out* of here," Frida said forcefully, thrusting a foot in the stirrup and swinging up into Ocelot's saddle.

"Glad you and me decided to come along, for backup, huh?" Rob said to her.

Frida widened her eyes. "Speak for yourself, sir."

*

The squadron reached the bottom of the extreme hills without further incident and veered southwest. The adjacent foothills were coated with a light dusting of snow. As they rode along, Rob welcomed the enveloping shade and quiet of the cold taiga. He listened to the crunch of cart wheels on the snowy ground and watched Saber puff out frosty breaths.

The going was slow, with the pack train weaving in and around terrace blocks as the terrain continued to decline. A few skeletons spawned in the low light, but Frida's and Rob's sharp lookout at the front and rear gave the troopers plenty of time to react and defend themselves. At last, they came out of the mountain zone, onto a flat, snowy expanse as slick as a child's slide, broken only by spruce trees. Fortunately, all of their animals were shod, and the cart wheels grabbed enough traction to spin.

The white carpet also highlighted any movement along the darkening trail. Turner spied a clutch of rabbits that saw them and attempted to hop away. He drew his bow, ammo, flint, and steel. Three short whispers through air were all Rob heard before a trio of flaming arrows met their marks. Instantly, the smell of cooked meat met his nostrils.

"Midnight snack, anybody?" Turner called.

The troopers ate on the move. They rode in pairs now, gnawing on rabbit parts and becoming talkative again as their food bars filled. Discussion turned to Frida's latest discovery with Crash in the Beta caverns.

"What would it take to mine every bit of gold from even one reach of that cave?" Frida mused. "I mean, you'd need some serious manpower. I don't see how anyone could've done that without our knowing."

Turner said, "Only living soul I know could do it is that crazy sister of De Vries's. Ever think of that?"

Frida shot him a glare. "She's on the level."

"If not her, though, then who?" Kim put in. "We have to ask ourselves if it's somebody we know. Could it be an inside job?"

The very thought made the captain queasy. The peace-loving cowboy wanted to think the best of people he met. Sure, he'd known his share of shifty types back in his old world. But this place . . . What with griefers and sorcerers and hostile mobs, the Overworld population leaned heavily toward characters who were less than truthful, or who'd just as soon kill you and take your stuff as say *howdy*. The healthy suspicion it took to evaluate folks' motives was simply not in Rob's toolbox.

That was why he appreciated Frida's survivalist skills. She made it her business to read people. "I know we went over this before, Vanguard. But now what do you think?" he asked her.

Frida had signed off on the integrity of Crash and her brother soon after they'd signed on with Battalion Zero—as travelers, before the Beta project had begun. But things could change. "I still get the same good vibes from our team," Frida said. "Maybe we ought to check up on the crew De Vries hired. He said he knew them from previous jobs, but what were they doing in the meantime?"

Kim said, "Lady Craven could've bribed them, or threatened them."

"Or both," Turner added. "That's how I'd do it."

Frida turned to raise eyebrows at him.

"Not that I would," he said abruptly.

It had been a long time since the sergeant had last tried to pad his inventory at the expense of his cavalry mates. Rob wondered if Turner's dark side was resurfacing. Still, the virtuous commander preferred deduction to suspicion and did not rush to judgment.

"A mole in camp would explain how somebody could plant that silverfish egg," Rob reasoned. "Lots of people heard me order a supply trip over the hills."

"But De Vries's construction crew was staying with *him*, in town," Frida said. "And I don't see how they would know about the gold strikes. Crash did all the mining on her own."

Turner grunted. "Bringin' us back to my original point. Bet it's her."

There was a pause. Nobody else wanted to think ill of the industrious miner.

In the silence, Rob heard a rumbling behind him. He halted Saber and Rat, to make sure the sound wasn't coming from the packhorse carts. He could make out distinct hoof beats. His body tensed.

"Squadron! To arms!" He felt something sharp press into his neck.

"*Too late.*"

Rob knew that voice.

"All o' youse. Drop yer weapons."

Rob drew back to see a blade aimed at his throat. Two riders hustled up on horses to join his captor, who held him at saber-point from the back of her own mount. In the final shards of daylight, the captain picked out a woman's sharp features.

"Precious," Rob said conversationally. "Fancy meeting you out here."

The troopers had halted and dropped their arms, but now Turner and Frida edged their horses toward Rob. They both recognized the rustler gang they'd run into twice before. A faint sound of bone clacking drifted through the darkening gloom, but the thieves were enjoying themselves and didn't pay the signal any mind.

Precious's two goons trained modified crossbows on the group.

"Git down," the leader ordered. "We'll be takin' them ponies now."

Rob, thinking to distract the griefers, said, "Well, only one of them is really a pony." He took his time dismounting. "Rat, here, is a hair too big. And you remember Norma Jean." Kim and Rob had appropriated both animals from the gang at their first encounter. "She's a horse-sized . . . *mule.*"

Rob reached out and clapped the mule on the rump. Norma Jean opened her mouth wide and bellowed with a series of outraged brays, followed by one very large gaseous explosion.

The smell and chaos covered the advance of a mixed band of skeletons and zombies, which had appeared suddenly and now attracted the bead of the rustlers' crossbows. This gave the troopers a chance to lunge for their inventories, where extra arms were stashed.

The melee that followed was a blur of moving targets as the combatants tried to decide which victim posed the greatest threat. Rob's marksmen, however, were more experienced than Precious's gang—and the skeletons and zombies were unable to multitask, let alone prioritize.

The squadron let the rustlers waste ammunition on the hybrid mob while they silently checked in with one another. Rob eyed Turner and cocked his head at the rustlers. Then he motioned for Frida and Kim to fall back with him, where they would have more room to wield their bows.

"Now!" he cried.

Turner let fly two stone axes, one at each of the goon's trigger fingers, sending their weapons sailing. Four skeletons fell on the disarmed men and killed them.

Seeing this, Precious wheeled her horse and galloped off. The last standing zombie lurched after her. Rob, Frida, and Kim engaged the remaining skeletons with arrow fire, taking the odd hit but firing faster and more surely. One final skull dropped to the ground before the hoof beats of Precious's horse and the zombie's cries had faded away.

"After her!" Rob yelled. "We can't let her get away this time."

He and Kim left the pack train there. The four riders grabbed the weapons they'd dropped and lit out after the fleeing rustler, moonlight now glinting off the snowy ground to show the way. They followed the dark tracks in the snow at a flat-out run until, at last, they heard the sound of a galloping horse moving up ahead. Precious and her mount must have shaken the zombie.

"She's mine!" Turner called, urging Duff past Ocelot.

Then Frida noticed the hoof tracks cut off to the left. "No, wait! Turner, don't!"

Before she could rein in Ocelot or warn the others, Turner and Duff suddenly dropped from sight. Saber, Ocelot, and Nightwind could not stop, and ran after them. Suddenly, Rob felt Saber fall out from under him. Then his own body tumbled forward, out of the saddle. It rolled through midair as though catapulted from a giant slingshot.

The horrible memory of another unexpected fall—from thirty thousand feet and the comfort of his coach seat—flitted through his mind. Only, this time, his scream had company.

Then the lights went out.

CHAPTER 9

THE HORSES' MOVEMENTS JOSTLED ROB BACK TO consciousness. Something cold and wet filled his eyes and nose. He snorted along with the animals, which were getting to their feet. A quick pat down of his own arms and legs showed some fall damage, but the snowy landing must have minimized it.

"Aaugh!"

"Turner?" Rob couldn't see much. A heavy bower of spruce trees sliced the moon's rays to slivers.

"Get off my foot, you knot-headed beast!" It sounded as though the sergeant had entangled himself with a horse.

"S-squadron?"

"Here, sir," came Frida's voice. This helped Rob distinguish her shape in the gloom.

Kim checked in and struggled to stand nearby. Turner swore soundly at the pain. Rob heard the horses blowing and swaying restlessly, but there seemed to be nowhere for them to go. They had plunged into a hole of some type.

"Vanguard! Can you get a look out?"

"I'll try," Frida said, groping about in the dark for Ocelot to use as a step stool. But the mare's saddle had turned "turtle" in the fall, and Frida's snow-dampened hands could not work the girth straps to right it.

"I'll boost you up on Nightwind," Kim offered. "He's the tallest, anyway."

Frida shimmied into the stallion's saddle and stood up, putting out her hands to feel for a ledge in front of her. She found purchase and pulled herself up a ways.

"See anything?" Turner asked.

"Seems to be a classic pit trap, folks. Broken spruce branches must've covered the top. It all caved in when Duff hit it."

"So, now it's my fault," the sergeant said defensively.

"We ran at it blind," Rob asserted. "Could've been any one of us."

Frida dropped down next to him. "It's a good thing Jools didn't build the trap, or we'd all be shish kebabs right now."

"Well, at least two of us would've respawned back in camp," Kim said. "Doesn't that give you food for thought?"

Frida said nothing.

"Ain't you lot high and mighty?" Turner groused. "Bet you're about to say you told me so, eh, Captain?"

Rob hesitated. "I'd think a near-death experience would be all the telling you needed."

"Can we stop second-guessing things and work on getting out of here?" Frida said crossly.

There was a rustling, and then a beam of light illuminated the pit. Rob saw Turner's face in the glow of a yellow leather miner's cap he was adjusting on his head.

"I borrowed it," Turner explained, catching Rob's disapproving stare. "I'll give it back."

"Sure you will."

In this case, though, they were all grateful for Turner's light fingers. The headlamp allowed them to find the weapons they'd dropped and let Frida attend to Ocelot's saddle.

Kim surveyed their prison. "We could probably all climb out, but the horses'll need help."

"'Fraid I'll need some help, too," Turner said. "Duff's mangled up my foot somethin' awful."

Rob winced. Getting stepped on was no fun. "Fortunately, you don't need two feet to ride."

Kim returned to solving the problem at hand. "If the rest of us all move into one corner, someone can mine out a wall of snow blocks and stack 'em to form a ramp."

"I'll do it," Rob said. He borrowed a diamond axe from Turner and got started.

The captain made short work of the wall and began stacking a sloping terrace that the animals could navigate. Meanwhile, in their corner, the horses stamped and fussed—but the three troopers holding them kept well away from their hooves. Then Ocelot's head went up, and she gave a long, shrill whinny.

As if in answer, low moans crescendoed: "Uuuuhh . . . *ooohh* . . . *ooohh*! Turner swung his headlamp up to reveal a line of zombie heads bobbing at the edge of the pit. A familiar stench drifted downward.

Rob's stomach tightened with fear. He had just built the zombies a staircase!

The first two mobsters lurched down the ramp and took swipes at him.

"*Oof!*"

Before Rob could get to his sword, another set upon him and began gnawing on his arm. He screamed and backed away, but all three zombies clutched at him. Rob could see the flaps of their rotting flesh swinging back and forth, wafting the stink of death into the pit.

Suddenly, Frida was there, silently slitting the feeding zombie's throat. Rob shook his mauled arm to loose its clenched teeth, which rotted away to nothing.

"Die! Die! Die!" yelled Kim, throwing herself at the other two monsters as she wielded a golden axe in each hand. She kept chopping even after they'd expired, turning their dropped potatoes into french fries.

But in came another wave.

"Get down!" yelled Turner, and the other three troopers dropped to the ground. With the frightened horses milling and half-rearing behind him, he knelt on his bad leg and sent arrow after arrow at the hideous foes, knocking off flesh until what little remained could no longer support their beings.

The gruesome noise stopped.

Again, the four troopers waited in shock, to be sure that the battle had ended.

Rob slowly regained his footing. "Good shooting, Sergeant," he said as Turner, exhausted, lost his balance and toppled over. Frida went to help him sit up against the snow wall.

Kim did what she could to pacify the horses. Then, she threw Saber's and Duff's reins to Rob and motioned for him to follow her, Nightwind, and Ocelot up the snow ramp and out to level ground. Frida acted as a human crutch for the injured Turner, and soon the group had gathered at the edge of the pit trap, free once more.

No one could afford a bout of food poisoning, so the zombies' rotten flesh was left behind. As the horses nosed in the snow for hidden grass, Rob and the rest hungrily chewed on raw potato bits. This restored their health somewhat—they'd all sustained a lot of damage after the fall and zombie hits. But Rob knew they were still vulnerable. Another attack like that and he'd wish he had changed his spawn point when he'd had the chance.

After the quick meal, Kim volunteered to go searching for Rat and Norma Jean while Rob and Turner rested.

"I'll go with you," Frida said. She checked Ocelot's girth one more time before getting back in the saddle, and the two young women rode off.

Meanwhile, the sergeant and captain leaned up against two spruce trees, their bows and arrows handy. Turner rubbed his ankle. "Wish I could pull my boot off," he complained.

"Do that and you might never get it back on," Rob said. "If only Jools were here with his brewing inventory. Or some milk. Then we could eat that pile of zombie flesh."

"Said the man who once caught a pufferfish in his teeth!" Turner was referring to the day they'd met Jools, when the cowboy was still a newbie and thought food poisoning would kill a healthy man.

Rob chuckled. "Remember when I didn't know the difference between a ghast and a magma cube?"

Turner laughed. "I can't believe you lived long enough to find out. Or stuck it out this long," he said more seriously.

Rob contemplated those early days. "I thought I'd find my way out of here in about two weeks. And yet, I'm still here."

"Now you've changed your spawn point, I reckon the Overworld'll be your new address."

Rob didn't reply.

Turner squinted at him sideways. "You did . . . change your spawn point."

"Of course I did," Rob said too vehemently.

"Of course you did," Turner said, and fell silent.

*

A short while later, the creaking of wheeled carts announced the girls' return. Nightwind and his rider stepped into view, followed by Norma Jean and her string of carts. "Hello in camp!" called Kim. "We got 'em, Captain."

Frida, however, led an unencumbered Rat. They had found the packhorse sweaty and trailing a broken harness, his carts lying in pieces along the path. Kim sorted through the wreckage, which they'd tossed into the mule's wagon. "If you all can wait, I think I can fix these," she said.

While Kim worked, the other troopers hung out, idly chatting and occasionally swatting at spiders that crawled or jumped by. The first soft rays of sunlight eased through the tree cover as the repairs were finished. Rob noticed that he wasn't even tired.

I'm getting used to not needing sleep, he thought, and then grimaced. What he needed to do was sleep in a bed—and not just to get his beauty rest. Deceiving his troops was about as low as he could go. "Mount up!" he ordered. The sooner they picked up their groceries, the sooner he could make amends.

With the sun rising and their food bars stabilized, the players and their equine friends found new energy. They made good time, soon reaching the "three corners" point where the cold taiga met mountain and mega taigas, a short distance from their destination. Rob couldn't help but climb down from Saber and play with the biome boundaries.

"Look! I'm in the cold taiga. No, wait! The mega taiga." He lay down on the spot. "I'm in three biomes at once. . . ."

The others tolerated his antics, glad to see their captain in a better mood.

Once they crossed into the hilly savanna, the landscape came alive with grazing animals. Pigs and chickens trotted by. Rabbits pulled at grass and stared at the horses and riders. Loose herds of cows and sheep appeared to be waiting for something to happen.

Turner, mounted on Duff with his foot hanging out of the stirrup, dropped his reins and drew a weapon in each hand. "Let's get busy, folks!" he said, urging his horse forward at a canter. The peaceful cattle in his path didn't see him as a threat. His iron sword and diamond axe flashed like sushi knives until four cows had become ingredients for four cowhide rugs and a stack of steaks.

Meanwhile, Frida launched Ocelot at a flock of sheep. Her quick swordplay reduced them to mutton, and spun and knit their wool into darling scarves, which she distributed among her friends.

"I got a pink one!" Turner cooed, getting a jealous look from Kim.

Rob and Kim took breaks from leading the pack animals to stalk and kill mobs of chickens and pigs that came close. "Leave the babies!" Kim said, knowing they wouldn't drop anything edible until they were more fully grown.

Their inventories bursting, the troopers ceased hunting and headed across the boundary into the plains. They found Swale's old farm and traded a dozen emeralds for huge stacks of wheat, which they piled into some of the empty wagons. Then the group set out for the flower forest, just over the border, where the pumpkin farmer lived.

Revisiting places he'd been before drove home to Rob how familiar the Overworld was becoming. Not so long ago it had all been the great unknown. Now, he was looking up "old" friends—or, at least, folks who weren't complete strangers.

"Welcome! You're back!" The wizened woman who ran the pumpkin operation seemed starved for company. They found her in the fields, dressed in the same soiled green coveralls and orange, wide-brimmed sun hat. A string of pumpkin seeds around her neck might have been her lunch. "What can I do for you today?" she asked. It was the same sweet reception she'd given them before.

Rob wondered if she knew that the harvest they'd forcibly taken from her had gone toward Bluedog's criminal pursuits. This time, though, they were paying for the exchange. At her invitation, the riders tied up their horses and took in the maturing pumpkin crop.

After talking business, the farmer pushed her sun hat back on her head and hiked up her coveralls. She punched a thumb at Turner. "You're the growing boy who likes my pie so much. You must come up to the house for some."

Turner had helped himself to more than his fair share of pie on the last visit. He slid his eyes toward Rob, then back at the farmer. "Well, thank you kindly, ma'am. I am enjoyin' a growth spurt these days."

The woman wheeled off for the clapboard farmhouse at a pace that left the limping sergeant in the dust.

"Frida? A hand here?"

The vanguard, remembering Turner's earlier appalling behavior at the farm, ignored him and kept marching. By the time he caught up, the farmer had already shown the others her flower garden and ushered them inside.

They sat around a plank table, enjoying slabs of pumpkin pie and goblets of flower water. Rob felt the life flow back into him, and he drifted off in a mellow daydream. A snippet of conversation brought his attention back to the table.

". . . you folks heard that the syndicate is building a new city?"

"Huh?" Rob sat up straight. "You mean, the UBO. The UBO is building a capital city. To unify all the biomes."

The woman appeared certain. "No, no. It's those nice syndicate folks who were protecting my land from those awful griefers. A messenger come riding by a while back, wanting donations to the cause."

Frida eyed Rob, then asked the woman, "You didn't give them anything, did you?"

"Well, I give 'em a load of squash, and fifteen emeralds."

"Did ya now?" Turner said, suddenly more interested in what she had to say.

"Weren't much. But it was all I had."

Turner put down the piece of crust he was about to eat. "Say, ma'am. You wouldn't want to donate to our cause, too, would ya? We've got a heck of a city goin' up—"

Rob cut him off. "We'll pay for the pumpkins, fair and square," he said firmly, rising from the table. "Who was it you said came by looking for charity, ma'am?"

"Now let me see . . . what was his name? Bolt? Colt?"

The troopers glanced at each other, showing no signs of recognition.

"Volt! He called himself Volt. Said he'd be back."

Frida patted the woman's shoulder. "I wouldn't give him any more resources, though. I hear your biome is going to join the UBO."

The woman absorbed this information. She smiled. "Well, isn't that lovely?"

*

The troopers rode off, back toward the cold taiga, digesting the news along with their pie. Aswan had mentioned that the syndicate had gone underground. The thieves looked to be keeping a low profile as they refilled the treasure chests that the battalion had emptied for them.

"You don't think they're really planning to stake a claim on the Overworld, do you?" Kim asked. She knew that anything the rogue griefers had told the farmer was suspect.

"I think nothing's changed," Rob answered. "I'll bet they're still stealing loot in Lady Craven's name, and taking a large cut of it, plus whatever favors she might grant them."

"D'you think Precious was in on it?"

"Maybe. I don't think she's got the guts to pull off anything big on her own. She's working for somebody else."

"She didn't want to steal our horses to trade," Kim realized.

"Not for the gems they'd bring," Frida agreed. "They're more valuable to us than to her."

"That's it," Turner said. "Somebody knew takin' our horses would cause a spiral effect on the Beta project. No horses, no food hauled back. No vittles, no workers."

Rob frowned. "So, whoever hired Precious . . . and this Volt character, is in league with the griefer army. We still don't know whether Lady Craven is directing them, or where she is."

"Or who might be leaking information from the jobsite," Frida said. "That's our Achilles' heel."

"Speakin' of heels . . ." Turner scowled. "I could use a potion right about now."

"We could hit Spike City for the night, and you could trade for some healing elixir," Kim suggested.

"I would . . ." the sergeant said dubiously, "but I'd have to borrow some scratch until I get paid."

"We've used up our expense account on these goods," Rob said shortly.

"Don't look at me, Meat," Frida warned Turner.

"Kim? How's about you spot me a few gems?"

"Sorry, Sarge. I'm saving up for something special." She paused. "Why not just change your spawn point, like the captain asked? Does it really matter where in the world a man like you hits the ground? There'll always be work for a weapons expert such as yourself."

"Not if someone switches game modes behind my back. Windin' up in Peaceful mode's my biggest nightmare." He shuddered. "Nah . . . a man's spawn point oughta be kept private."

"Even if other people's lives depend on it?" Kim prodded.

Turner maintained a sour silence.

Rob needled the mercenary, "And, don't forget about Rose. She's reason enough to return to Beta, even if the rest of us aren't." He realized what he'd said and cast a guilty glance at Frida up ahead. If there was anyone the cavalry commander would not want to lose—in this life or the next—it was her.

CHAPTER 10

ATHER THAN BRING MORE PRESSURE DOWN ON himself, Turner suffered the remainder of the trip back to Beta without complaint. The squadron rode on through the night, fending off the usual hostile mobs. Rob preferred a sure fight to a meeting with questionable strangers any day.

Although they didn't stop as they passed Spike City, Rob noted that the dislocated minecart tracks had been repaired and rerouted to the village's back door. He half-expected to see the Thunder Boys zoom past. But the only disruptions on the journey north-and-upward came from zombies, a few skeletons, and two lost-looking endermen. The cavalry team skirmished their way toward dawn, avoiding contact only with the neutral endermen. Rob finally felt his energy drain away. When morning broke and the riders could see

Beta in the distance, the group fell into a tense quiet, unsure of who—or what—they would find there this time.

To Rob's amazement, they rode into a city buzzing with happy industriousness. People literally whistled while they worked, and no one appeared to be idle. As folks spied the cartloads of wheat and pumpkins and inventoried meats that the squadron carried, joyous cries went up.

Then, suddenly, the pack train was surrounded. Frontrunners in the crowd grabbed onto the wagons before they rolled to a stop. One settler frantically emptied his hotbar, intending to stuff it with stacks of food.

"Not so fast there, compadre!" Turner addressed him. "This ain't no self-service buffet," he warned, reining Duff back toward Rat's flank.

When the villager ignored the order and reached for a pumpkin, Turner dropped the reins and drew his two diamond axes from their shoulder holsters. The sharp blades glistened in the morning sun. Both men engaged in a standoff as wrist and axe stopped just short of contact. Then the settler gingerly withdrew, giggling nervously.

Turner puffed his chest out, axes still aloft. "Now, that *was* funny. Sharpest tool known to man nearly meets . . . meat."

The settler slunk away.

Turner glared at the others in the crowd who were all cringing. "Anyone else?" There were no takers. "That's what I thought."

The crowd parted and the pack train continued to the center of town and stopped at the community well. Rob was pleased to see an iron golem chained to it, on guard. Without any prompting, those assembled formed an orderly line, just as Jools and Stormie caught up with the incoming party.

"That's it: queue up!" Jools called. "Everybody gets a ration, as soon as I take stock." He pulled out his computer and began to log items into his spreadsheet.

"Wonderful to see you, Bat Zero!" Stormie greeted them more cheerfully than the last time Rob rode in. *She must have good news*, he thought. *About time.*

"Everything going well, Artilleryman?" he asked as Frida, Kim, and Turner nodded hello.

"Coming up roses, Captain, since y'all left."

Turner frowned at her. "You sayin' *we're* the bad luck charm?"

Stormie drew back, puzzled.

"He's got an owwie," Kim explained. "Feeling sorry for himself."

Now Turner gave her a dark look. "I'll be in my quarters," he grumbled and turned Duff back toward the gate.

Meanwhile, Jools finished his list and let the settlers in line pass by, taking half a stack of their choice, for a snack to hold them and their families until the cook's bell.

"Come see the new developments," Stormie urged the captain.

Rob let Kim and Frida take the remaining supplies and horses down to camp, while he and Jools joined the artilleryman, whose bright mood was infectious.

The after-effects of damage and fatigue that Rob had experienced on the trail were forgotten as the comforting feeling of being on home turf returned. His step showed a definite spring as he and Stormie walked down the developing main street, which was looking far less war-weary than it had before. Cobblestone paving and transplanted shrubbery refined the scene, while the adjacent building projects had moved beyond the skeleton stage. Solid foundations and rising walls hinted at what the actual finished structures would be like.

De Vries emerged from the job office and headed toward the cavalry mates.

"Farm's back online," Stormie pointed out as the builder caught up with them. Leafy green seedlings and a sparkling waterfall had replaced the black tar pit Rob had last seen there, lending a hopeful air to the entire site.

"But how—?"

"You can thank the Thunder Boys," Jools replied before Rob could finish forming the question. "Preliminary run on the new rails. Swale replaced the baby plants in exchange for the first ride."

They set off toward the hillside, which marked the city's eastern boundary. The commercial center was still only plotted out. But the new high-rise apartments were almost finished, Rob saw as they neared the rising cliffside. De Vries bubbled with pride at their design.

"Backed against the hills, these buildings will make very secure shelters," the architect explained. "They'll face a lovely park here"—he pointed at the open space at their front doors—"and the view! It's an eye-popper."

It would have to be, at twenty blocks higher than the steep hillside. The towers would certainly rival the finest ice-spike condominiums. Rob goggled at the skyscrapers.

"There's a penthouse with your name tag on it, Captain," De Vries offered. "And one each for the judge and colonel. You fellows have earned it."

Rob ducked his head in shame, appearing more modest than unworthy. "Aw, I'm more of a stars-and-bedroll kinda guy, anyway," he mumbled.

"Well, I'm not," Stormie cut in.

Rob eyed her. "Since when?"

"Oh, lately," she said, nonchalantly. "Sleep in a bed these days, sir."

Rob stopped short in the street. "You—what?"

"Sleep in a bed now," she repeated. "I need the money." She was obviously teasing him.

This only made Rob feel more guilty. "I'll see your pay is drawn up at once," he said.

She shook her head. "I'll take it end of the month, same as normal, Captain. Now that my arsenal is built up, I've got everything I need." She waved at the men and women working on the nearly completed apartment dwellings. "Seein' these people move in and get comfy'll be payment of its own."

*

Stormie's new role, bringing people together, seemed at odds with her facility for blowing things up. Yet— Rob had to admit—her heart was in the right place, just as his own passion proved to be elusive. What was it Colonel M had asked him to do? Delve into his reasons for loving his old work, his old life. . . . Rob hadn't had a moment alone to work all that out.

He was about to excuse himself and seize that moment when Jools and De Vries asked him to tour the minecart roundhouse and high-rise interiors.

Rob said, "I'll take a rain check. Saber and I need to get some rest. It was a . . . demanding trip. You'll get my full report at tomorrow's meeting. Then I can devote my attention to your creations. Meanwhile, Jools, tell me: how are you handling our Thunder Boys? So the suspense won't kill me." He managed a tired smile.

Now the quartermaster scrutinized the captain, who did appear to need a lie-down. "Suffice it to say, sir, that we've had a meeting of the minds."

They exchanged satisfied glances, and Rob wandered off, bound for cav camp. In just a few days, the settlers would be able to vacate the tent city. Until then, though, privacy would be at a premium. To get it, Rob realized he'd need a disguise.

On his way out of the build site, he liberated a torch from the farm and a pumpkin from the official stores, and quickly crafted a jack-o'-lantern. He stuck it on his head. Then he removed his chaps and vest and tucked them under his arm, returning to camp in his shirtsleeves and jeans—utter anonymity.

The mission had, indeed, been hard on the horses— long climbs over the extreme hills, the fall into the pit trap, and errant swipes by zombies. Rob decided to take Saber out for a restorative stroll, for both of their sakes.

The stallion snorted when the pumpkin-headed captain entered the pasture, but settled down upon catching his true scent. Rob clipped a lead rope on his horse, and the pair crossed the drawbridge without any special notice. Then they headed for the edge of camp.

When they reached the area where the battalion had lain in wait for skeletons some nights before, Rob removed his disguise. "Alone at last," he murmured to Saber, allowing him to put his head down and graze at will. Grass grew in tufts at this elevation, but the steep terrain discouraged other grazing animals from spawning here. Saber's rhythmic pull and chew on the grass soon lulled the cowboy-at-heart into the calm mood he'd sought.

Rob let his mind slide backward—past the Beta project, before the battles with Lady Craven and Dr. Dirt, before his sudden drop into the ocean— and into his old "normal." Those days had begun and ended with a herd check and had been colored by Mother Nature's terror and beauty. He'd never sought that life—he had been born into it. Shown the way by folks who'd gone before him . . . folks who'd simply assumed it was the life for him. *Funny*, Rob mused. *Ya think everyday normal will never end.* He marveled that humans are both blessed and cursed by an inability to see around the next corner.

Saber, tugging on the rope, led Rob a few more paces toward the line of rocks at the edge of the flat clearing. He noticed the ground harden beneath his feet, and then he heard a distinctive *click!* He'd stepped on a pressure plate.

Rob froze. There was no telling what the device might trigger.

Saber, wanting some morsels that were just out of reach, pulled at the lead rope again. Rob had no choice but to drop it and let the horse go.

Before he could call out or come up with another course of action, he heard noise—a chittering sound he'd heard before, like the silverfish made. *Do endermites make that sound?* he wondered, alarmed. He dared not turn around for fear of disturbing the pressure plate.

Then he heard breathing—human-type breathing—and the hiss-clicks stopped.

"I've been waiting to find you alone," came a low voice so calm, yet so full of crazy, that Rob's blood ran even colder.

"Wh-what d'you want with me?" He tried not to shake in his boots. A thin trickle of sweat ran down his back.

"*Hyeh, hyeh, hyeh . . .*" A quiet, evil laugh met Rob's ears.

No one was witnessing this. No one but he could hear what was going on. Even the happily grazing Saber had wandered far enough down the dry runoff path that he didn't notice an intruder or whinny in alarm.

"Don't move, now," the unidentified creature said.

Rob fought for control. What would he have done in his old world? There, he'd always had an example of bravery to follow: Jip swimming against the current to turn a wayward calf; Pistol using teeth, and hooves, and his strong neck muscles to stun and fling away a striking snake. At the very least, when faced with near-impossible danger, they'd refused to show fear.

Rob grasped for that weapon now. "Who are you?" he demanded. "You'll never get away with this," he added, sounding much more certain than he was.

"Getting away doesn't interest me," Rob's captor remarked. I'm perfectly comfortable in this nice, new city that you're building. It's you who'd like to get away now."

"Let me go! Or a dozen armed and armored soldiers will have your head," Rob threatened.

"Hyeh, hyeh, hyeh . . ."

That laugh! Nothing could be more terrifying than a laugh with no humor in it.

"Your city will stand—as a target," promised the kidnapper.

"For who?" Rob demanded as sweat soaked through his clothing.

"For every dark force in and under the Overworld. Unless . . ."

"Unless, what?"

"Unless you cease your plot to take over the biomes."

"*Our* plot? We're here to unite the biomes, not conquer them," he said, angry now. Battalion Zero's message had been clear all along: the only acceptable Overworld was a free Overworld.

"You lie."

"I never lie," Rob fibbed.

"Here's what you *will* do. You will stop trying to enslave the poor village people of these biomes. And you will tell no one why."

"Or, what?"

"Or those soldiers you hold in such high regard will die." The voice swam with wicked intent. "What is the name of that little, green one you like so much?"

Rob's stomach puckered. He didn't answer.

"The one who comes from the jungle, who kept you alive when you were powerless as an ocelot kitten. . . . Her name does not matter. *Hyeh, hyeh, hyeh . . .* And it will fade away—just a glitch in the game program— if you do not leave the biomes' fate to the powers that be."

Rob fished for clues. "What powers? The people are the ones with the power now—or they will be, once the biomes stand together again."

"You want to see power?" The question ended in a high note that spelled madness—and held a clear threat.

Rob waited. He expected to hear an explosion or see some hideous monster conceived in his nightmares leaping out at him.

But he only heard a *click.*

"*I* have the power. The power to release you. Which I will do, at the count of ten."

Then came the dreadful chittering sound again, and then . . . nothing.

Rob counted to ten. Did he dare step off the pressure plate?

Death had never seemed so near, or so complicated, before.

Just then, he heard hoof beats, and a startled-looking Saber ran into view. The horse gave a worried nicker.

Well, if I go, we go together, Rob thought, stumbling backward.

There was no explosive report, no flood of arthropods, no pain . . . no evidence that anyone had been there, Rob realized, as he checked the immediate area. *But I can't tell a soul. The others are in danger. Frida's in danger! It'll be my fault if they're harmed.*

What better reason could the cavalry commander have to change his spawn point now . . . and not to change it? Yes, he owed it to his friends—to Frida—to be here for them, at ground zero. Then again, high-tailing it home might be the smartest thing Rob could do.

*

The cowboy struggled for perspective. How would his role models respond if they were in his shoes? He knew that horses met a defensive attack by going into fight mode. But, when threatened by a formidable predator, they'd enter flight mode. The ones that ran and didn't look back might succeed. Those that faltered, probably wouldn't. Rob decided that the only way to carry this extra burden in front of his troops was to put one foot in front of the other, and fix his sights on the horizon.

Getting Battalion Zero riled up wouldn't do them any good, Rob figured, until he could learn who was behind the intimidation. This was no time to be making big personal decisions, either. There was too much to think about. For now, the horses' example would have to get the captain through the day—and night.

Rob tucked his bedroll under his un-slept-in bed the next morning and went out to suffer through everyone else's jolly mood. He grimaced at the strains of classical guitar music drifting through camp, and the happy shouts of children playing. The battalion's good-natured banter at breakfast made him feel slightly ill. *They're so darn cheerful.* Rob had come to depend on the unit facing risks together. He was remembering how lonely his job could be.

As if to underscore his situation, Turner and Rose, and Frida and Gratiano, invited him to walk with them to the build site. A Beta project meeting and high-rise tour were on tap. "Double dating?" Rob couldn't help asking.

Turner wrapped an arm around Rose's waist. "Lonesome, Cap'n? I can get you a blind date. Ladies love an officer, you know."

Rose snuggled closer to him, and he winced, exaggerating his limp.

"You do know he's just a noncommissioned officer, right?" Rob pointed out rudely.

Turner sniffed. "Who cares? Don't need to go to some academy to learn what comes natural to me. Besides, noncoms got half the responsibility and all of the charm."

Rob knew better than to argue with Mr. Right. He hustled on ahead of the others.

The group stopped in at the jobsite trailer to pick up De Vries and Jools. Rose gave De Vries a meaningful look. Then she pecked Turner on the cheek, leaving a purple lipstick imprint. "Crash and I'll meet you at the apartments, gentlemen." She went into one of the offices and didn't come out.

Seeing Rob's inquisitive expression, De Vries spoke up, in his musical lilt. "I did as you asked, Captain. I handed off the interior planning to Rose. I've been taking lessons in delegating tasks from Jools." He grinned.

Jools said, "Yes, well. He's finding that it is possible to give up an iota of control without having it surgically removed."

"That's progress, all right," Rob acknowledged.

"Oh, there's more than that," De Vries said. "He's got me sleeping now."

Rob shot Jools a look. It was well known that the workaholic builder never slept.

"Had to lock in my spawn point at the jobsite," De Vries explained. "I admit, I've not had such long-term employment. Lead architect, project manager . . . it's all a huge responsibility."

"And Crash?" Rob asked.

"That *knor*? She's obsessed. My sister, the ore nerd, always makes sure to respawn wherever she's dug her tunnels."

Rob felt as though someone were battering him like a piñata. *One foot in front of the other*, he reminded himself. They went next door to city hall to chezck in with the judge and colonel.

Beta's officiates were busy playing an Overworld trivia game in the conference room. During some rare free time, the venerable man and the venerable man's head had found out they shared a vast knowledge of petty history.

"'In what version were wither skeletons first identified?'" Judge Tome read aloud.

"Oh, please," boomed Colonel M. "One-point-four-point-two. Ask me something harder, why don't—" He smiled at the visitors. "Troopers. Gentlemen. Do come in. Back from the wars, eh, Captain?"

Rob hesitated. "Feels like it, sir."

Judge Tome leaned forward. "I am itching for news from the real world. I never thought I would miss riding with the battalion so much."

"Then why don't you join our next training?" Rob glanced at De Vries. "And you and your sister, too."

"You never know when you'll need to be on your toes," Frida added. "It'll be fun."

They decided they would.

Kim and Stormie arrived, and Rob asked Frida to fill in the others on their supply mission. She recounted the intel and suspicion that had arisen. Hearing it all in one piece, the tale sounded harrowing, even to Rob.

Judge Tome frowned. "Let me see if I have this straight. Someone set a silverfish spawner to waylay your troops. When that didn't stop you, Precious and her men ambushed and then trapped you. Having escaped that, you wondered if the pumpkin farmer you traded with was in league with the griefer alliance. Is that right?"

Frida met his gaze. "I think she might know something she's not telling us."

Colonel M nodded. "I think she might."

"Meanwhile," the judge continued, "we've not had anything go missing here, nor suffered a plague of endermites."

"Nothing outside of the odd accident or typical bad luck on a build site," De Vries confirmed.

Then talk turned to the construction job status and, finally, to UBO business.

Colonel M addressed Frida and Rob. "We've finished our legal drafting. The new government has a framework, ready to be voted upon. We're waiting for you to canvass the next six biomes for members, as you had planned."

Rob stared at him dumbly.

"That's why you found us playing tiddlywinks when you walked in," Judge Tome explained.

"Stormie and I have the unification roster," Frida said. "We'll ride out to get those signatures whenever the captain's ready."

Rob nodded vaguely.

Jools spoke up. "Now, lads. To the minecart project!"

"To the high-rise project," De Vries countered.

Turner rose. "How's about, to lunch? My food bar's considerable low on chicken legs."

"Speaking of chicken legs . . ." Jools taunted, mimicking Turner's limp. "I've seen baby zombie chickens with a bolder stride."

With that, Turner lunged at him, but the quartermaster simply sidestepped the injured man and walked out the door.

CHAPTER 11

ROB SLEPT DEEPLY NEXT TO HIS BED AND AWOKE to a babel of voices outside the bunkhouse. When he could distinguish only Jools's clipped diction, Rob knew he could no longer put off meeting the Thunder Boys. He emerged from the cavalry quarters just as a light rain began to fall, which saved him washing up.

"To the rear, march!"

At the quartermaster's order, six leather-clad tribesmen marched off in six different directions. Settlers going about their business dodged them.

"No, no, no!" Jools cried, pulling at his close-cut hair. "Like this, Steve: watch!" He pushed several passersby into a line, spun the first one around, and urged the rest to follow the leader across the compound. The

Thunder Boys observed, pointing and debating the issue from behind their mirrored sunglasses.

"Where's your translator?" Rob asked Jools.

"Oh, *they* understand *me*. It's military logic they fail to comprehend."

Rob chuckled. "I can see that. But why are you training them?"

Jools sighed. "To keep them occupied. They're sharp as whips. They had the transit system together before you could say *bōsōzoku*."

"Well, we're going to need an infantry real soon. Do you think they'll get the hang of it?"

"If they don't drive me crazy first." He turned back toward the unruly foot soldiers. In the steady drizzle that ran off their hair and black leather suits, they resembled a troupe of performing sea lions. "Now, fall in! Let's try this again, for the captain's benefit."

Once Jools got them to form a ragged file, he marched them all out of camp. Rob followed them to the roundhouse, an area of the minecart tracks where a loop and side spurs had been added to allow turnarounds and to house the idle vehicles.

Jools introduced the Thunder Boys by occupation. "Steve, here, is our track inspector. This Steve maintains our existing fleet, while this Steve builds or modifies new carts. He's a bloody genius." The last

Steve dipped his mirrored sunglasses modestly. Jools continued, "These two Steves are night guards, and this Steve—" He hesitated. "What is it you do again?"

The minecart driver said something Rob didn't understand, and then pantomimed hands gunning a throttle.

"He's a driver. That's right. Refuses to do anything else, as of yet." Jools looked vexed.

"Good to know you, soldiers," Rob said, shaking hands all around. "The battalion and the UBO are grateful for your . . . expertise. I can honestly say that you six Steves probably know more about minecarts than I could learn in a lifetime."

They regarded him as though he were the most hopeless simpleton and exchanged murmurs of disbelief.

"Well, I'm—a cavalry and rodeo man from way back," Rob stammered, feeling as though he had to defend his manhood. "Don't suppose you all know much about bronc riding, do you?"

Again, the Thunder Boys consulted one another. Steve the driver pointed in the direction of the horse pasture and pretended to comb an invisible mane and tail.

Out of the corner of his mouth, Jools whispered, "I believe, sir, that they're pegging you as a groom."

Rob reddened. "There's more to it than that. . . ." He realized that an explanation was beyond them and gave up. "Carry on, men."

They immediately started shouting to each other and took off for their minecarts.

Jools watched them go. "Dismissed," he said wryly.

Meanwhile, Kim had arrived. She wore her pink cap today, to keep the rain off, and she carried an armload of halters and lead ropes. "Morning, Captain! Say, we've a shipment of saddle horses coming from Swale this afternoon."

"We're going to need them. I reckon we'll be amping up our cavalry numbers soon. Who's bringing the animals in?"

She grinned. "Me. Jools is letting me and Frida test out the new stock trailer." She pointed to one of the spur tracks in the roundhouse. In addition to the six modified minecarts, two new railcars sat waiting—one large, open-topped cart and one with benches and a roof. "Want to come along?" she asked. "There's plenty of room in the passenger cart."

The captain shook his head. "I promised De Vries I'd give the new apartments a walk-through." Rob secretly wanted to poke around the construction site for clues to the dangerous griefer he'd met. As distasteful as another encounter might be, he certainly didn't want to stray far from the city right now.

"We'll ride together tonight, then," Kim said. Rob had called for night training, hoping to lure any criminal elements out under cover of darkness.

"See you then," he said, ready to get in out of the rain.

Stormie saw the captain shaking off water and joined him, sharing her sapling umbrella as she fell into step. "Looking forward to tonight, sir," she said. "Good excuse to get my guns out." The artilleryman had finally accumulated enough material to practice firing her TNT cannon and redstone repeater.

"We'll give these townspeople a good show," Rob promised. He'd intended the armed drill to drum up interest in enlistments. Now, he hoped the show of force wouldn't be needed for defense.

"I'll be sure to save enough pops for some fireworks, down the line," Stormie said. "For the ribbon-cuttin' party."

If there is one, the commander thought. Still, at least the city was shaping up well, even if the UBO remained in pieces.

The iron golems gave the troopers yellow caps and let them pass through the main gate. Again, Rob wondered how a griefer was accessing the place. Was he in disguise? Using an underground entrance? The second possibility seemed worth pursuing. He'd find a moment to get Crash's opinion on the state of things in the mines.

As Rob and Stormie approached the site trailer, guitar music reached their ears. They entered to find Gratiano down on one knee, plucking another syrupy ballad for a rapt Rose. The decorator had a hypnotic way of locking eyes with a person when she wanted their attention—or, perhaps, something more. Fortunately, the accomplished musician could probably play in the dark, with a sack over his head and both hands tied behind his back . . . a position that Rob wouldn't mind seeing him in.

Gratiano finished his song and shook out his mane of curly hair in greeting, still enveloped in the decorator's mesmerizing stare.

"Frida otherwise engaged?" the captain asked, all but accusing the guitarist of infidelity.

"Turner down at the gym?" Stormie inquired, laying the same rap on Rose.

Rose slowly lifted her purple-fringed gaze from the handsome serenader. She ignored Stormie, and turned to address Rob. "I've sent De Vries for some more dyed wool. He'll meet us at the manors."

Rob raised eyebrows at Stormie. They could both see that the domineering woman had wrapped several men around her modified, purple-nailed finger.

Again, they took a diagonal shortcut through the city, passing the capitol compound, farm, and commercial district. The rain had stopped, and hot sun made a quick steam bath of the air. They arrived at the apartment complex just in time to see workers erect a huge sign embellished with a purple flower.

"'Rose Manor'?" Rob read aloud. "Who authorized this?"

"Oh, some of the higher-ups," Rose replied. "While you were off on your little pumpkin run."

This raised Stormie's hackles. "Squadron risked their lives to put meat on our tables. That's no pumpkin run."

"Artilleryman," Rob said, trying to extinguish her lit fuse. "Let's move on. We have weapons to clean when we're through here."

"Very, very *sharp* weapons, sir," Stormie said for Rose's ears. "And the kind that go *boom*."

Rose flinched, but didn't comment. De Vries met them at the entrance to ROSE 1, as the first building was labeled.

The builder carried an armload of magenta-and-mauve dyed wool. "Where do you want this stuff, Rosebud?"

She gazed at the top floor.

"For Rose's place," De Vries explained, with a helpless expression.

This did not sit well with Stormie. "*She* gets the other penthouse?"

Rose gave a smug smile. "Well, the captain didn't want it. . . ."

Rob could have cut the tension between the two women with a stone axe. They entered the building. Rose went upstairs to deliver her fabric while the others looked around.

Rob found the spruce paneling attractive and noted that the uniquely shaped windows let in light without allowing mobster access. He complimented De Vries on their design.

"They're die cut, using silk-touch shears," the builder said proudly. "The rose shape will repel everything but spiders, and we'll be hanging screens to keep them out."

"Safe," Rob murmured.

"Yet stylish," De Vries put in.

"Frida'll be tickled pink," Stormie said.

The decor was swanky, Rob had to admit. Red-and-black patterned wool draped a four-poster bed and easy chair, and matched the floor rug. A redstone-powered lamp, fireplace, and automatic window drapes were activated with a Clapper, which De Vries demonstrated. Rob noticed that the baseboards had a rough-hewn appearance. *Rustic chic. Modern.*

"This is nice, and all," Stormie mused, "but how come the bedroom's where the entry hall should be?"

De Vries thought a moment. "Didn't we go upstairs? I could've sworn—"

At that instant, Rose burst back into the room. "Devie! Someone's moved the view!"

The helpless look returned to De Vries's face, while suspicion hit Rob and Stormie at the same time.

"This oughta be the second floor. . . ." Stormie said.

Rob tried to make sense of the apparent rift in Overworld physics. "If the first floor's gone, then the penthouse is one story shorter! That's why the view has changed."

They both regarded love-struck De Vries, who was confounded by the reality of the situation. He sprang to the door and ran down the hall, opening more doors and shouting. He came back and reported the scene to the captain. The rustic portion of woodwork showed chew marks, and the building had somehow been cut off just there. The first-story entrance hall, manor office, and laundry room were simply gone.

"You're telling me something *ate* the ground floor?"

"Apparently so."

Baffled, Rob asked, "How the heck does something eat a whole floor of an apartment building?"

De Vries blinked at him. "In this case, I'd have to say, sir: one bite at a time."

*

The shaken captain interrupted the judge and colonel's trivia marathon for an impromptu meeting. Stormie summoned Crash from the mines and the rest of

Battalion Zero from camp. When they all assembled, De Vries relayed the shocking news.

The judge tried to wrap his mind around the possible causes. "Were there valuables stored on that floor?"

"Nothing yet," De Vries said. "It was mostly wood—wood walls, wood furniture; heck, wood in the fireplace, since we're not yet using lava."

Now Turner spoke up. "Wood, you say. . . . Anything else made of wood go missing? 'Cause I noticed my poker chips are gone."

Crash tapped her pickaxe on the stone conference table.

"There used to be a wooden table here," Kim recalled. The network computers it had held sat in a jumble on the floor, lights winking.

Stormie snapped her fingers. "We had to give the loggers iron axes because we ran out of wood ones awful fast. I didn't think they could all've broken."

Colonel M furrowed his massive brow. "I believe Sergeant Turner may be on to something."

Poor Judge Tome still couldn't get a handle on the strange predicament. "What—or who—consumes wood so voraciously and clandestinely?"

In answer, a long-ago vision flashed through Rob's mind, and he nearly blurted out what he was thinking. But he remembered the previous day's threat. He couldn't involve the others. He would have to remain silent until he could produce results—on his own.

Just then, Jools put up a hand. "Captain! Word from Aswan." He pushed his laptop computer to the center of the big table so the others could see.

The tradesman had no time for pleasantries. "I'll be brief. I don't know who might be listening," he said furtively. "I intercepted an encoded message from a man named Volt. I know of him. He's a small-time griefer who branched out when Bluedog left the area." Aswan checked over his shoulder. A commotion could be heard in another room.

"What did the message say?" Rob asked.

"It's not *what* but *where* that is important," Aswan corrected him.

"Why?"

The tradesman's voice sank to a whisper. "It was coming from your ten-forty."

Rob looked at Jools to interpret.

"That's cop for 'your location'!"

With a quick hail to Kim, Aswan signed off.

"*Volt* is the name the farmer gave us," Kim reminded everyone. "Remember? The griefer who was after 'donations'?"

Rob shivered. Was this the scoundrel he'd met the day before?

Judge Tome removed his eyeglasses and sat back in his chair. "So. *Fama volat.* Rumor travels fast, comrades. We now know that the Beta project does have a mole, probably going by the name of Volt. This person—or thing, in the absence of human evidence—may be linked to the disappearance of gold and wood from the site. He, she, or it may have access to monster eggs, knowledge of subterranean lava and water sources, and friends in the countryside from whom resources are being extorted." He rubbed the bridge of his nose. "None of this is adding up."

But it was, to Rob. All the captain could say to warn his friends, though, was, "Better safe than sorry, people. Judge. Colonel. I think we should all participate in drill tonight. Without a clear motive or target, any one of us could be next."

No one disagreed.

Jools got their attention again. "It's Gaia! Incoming message."

The Spike City church director's face filled the computer screen. "My friends. I hope you are well, for I've heard disturbing news from travelers through the village. Talk of unification has been met with . . . skepticism from outsiders, to put it lightly."

"Someone bad-mouthing the union?" Turner asked.

"We've heard from folks coming through the eastern biomes that the vote isn't going your way. They've received . . . threats."

Rob tensed. "What kind of threats?"

Gaia hesitated, then said, "Vague threats."

"Vague," Turner whispered through tight lips. "Them's the worst kind."

"Threats—coming from who?" Rob asked.

"From whom," Jools corrected in a whisper.

Turner gouged Jools with an elbow. "You swallow a dictionary?"

Rob ignored them. "Was the source clear?" he asked Gaia.

"Sorry to disappoint. It could be a rogue, someone working for the syndicate, or worse."

"Worse? Meaning the GIA?"

"They didn't say. . . . But the imperials are said to be holding a mushroom island in the eastern ocean. I don't know if there's any truth to that."

"But it's a clue," Rob said appreciatively. "You were right to let us know." This did add weight to yesterday's incident. Perhaps whoever had detained him had been threatening leaders in other biomes that were considering unification. "Thank you, Delegate. We'll be in touch."

"And if I might—" she put in. "How are my Thunder Boys doing?"

Jools answered, "Capital. There seems to be nothing they can't do. On the fifth try," he added under his breath.

"They're good boys," Gaia said and signed off.

This latest development left the group speechless for a few moments. Then Frida rose from the table. "I think it's time someone questioned our friend the pumpkin farmer. She claimed to have spoken to Volt directly."

"The job's yours," Rob said. "Take Turner with you. You can leave right after drill." He turned to Kim. "Corporal, buddy up with Stormie for your ride to Swale's place on the double. Bring those horses back here before dark." He got to his feet. "The rest of you, prep the weaponry and horses for training tonight. Attendance is mandatory. For you, too, Judge. Colonel, I hope you'll observe. I'll see you there. I've got something to take care of." He motioned for Crash to follow him outside.

*

The cowboy and the miner made their way to the hillside caverns. Rob told Crash he wanted to inspect the ore deposits, storage chests, and mining tunnels to see what he could find out.

As they entered the main mine cave, Crash stopped and looked around the stone room. Then she went and got a worker and pantomimed a question, pointing to the torches on the wall. She came back and let Rob know that redstone-powered lamps had been replaced with regular coal torches, and that she hadn't sanctioned the switch. Could Volt be targeting the redstone supplies? *That'd make sense*, Rob thought.

He asked Crash to lead him in the direction of the farm and the apartment complex, and she took off down a narrow corridor, swinging her pickaxe and leaving a trail of cobblestone and ore behind her. In one spot, she pointed upward and then acted out picking crops.

"The farm?" Rob guessed.

They stopped, and he saluted the alert settler who was guarding an aquifer in the rock that burbled out spring water. A stone canal zigzagged off, presumably toward the surface where it fed the farm irrigation system. Not far off lay a stagnant-looking lava pond. Someone who spent time underground might get the bright idea to tap into the water table from below and contaminate it with red-hot lava.

Rob nudged Crash. "Could this creek bed be excavated any further?"

She allowed that it could, since the artesian spring couldn't exist atop bedrock. The pair moved on.

"Let me know when we reach the apartment houses overhead," Rob said.

When Crash halted again and pointed upward, Rob noticed a honeycomb network split off from the main tunnel they were in. A person couldn't fit into the small holes in the rock . . . but a tinier creature could. Say, an arthropod.

"That's all I needed to see, Private," Rob told the miner. "Thanks." He paused a moment, listening, but heard nothing out of the ordinary. Still, someone—or something—had been here, and up to no good, Rob was sure of it.

He made up his mind to return later, alone.

CHAPTER 12

THE CAVALRY COMMANDER MET THE MINECART train at the roundhouse. Passenger and stock cars were sandwiched between two of the modified carts, with one Steve acting as conductor and another serving as lookout in the caboose. The contraption slowly pulled into the terminus. Above the platform where Rob stood, Jools leaned out of a six-block-high control tower, overseeing the other Steves. They busied themselves throwing switches and placing ramps for offloading the commuters and horses.

Before anyone could disembark, Rob entered the passenger car and spoke quietly to Kim. He gave her something from his inventory, then sat down on a bench to wait while the others unloaded.

The trackside activity shielded the arrival of an extra passenger, whom Kim escorted to the bunkhouse without notice. She returned to the train as Rob had asked, handing him his jack-o'-lantern mask. He put it on and wore it to the horse pasture, making a show of removing it so he wouldn't frighten the new animals that Kim and Frida had collected. They all joined Stormie and Turner to welcome the horses to their new home.

"Redstone!" Rob called, recognizing Josie's youngster. "You've grown."

Kim walked the filly in a circle to show her off.

"She's going to be big—" Rob predicted, "taller than her mama, I'll bet."

Kim started to lead her across the drawbridge, but the young horse broke away, eyed the moat, and then leapt it handily.

"She's already a good jumper," Kim said, stating the obvious.

"And not afraid of water," Rob put in.

"Or super-sharp Punji sticks," Jools added. "She might be my kind of horse, once she's trained."

Beckett raised his head from the pasture grass and gave an indignant whinny. Then he walked over to Redstone and nuzzled her a bit.

"Maybe she'll rub off on him," Rob said to Jools. He ordered Kim to prep the horses for night drill and Turner to distribute weapons. "Call me when the others get here. I'll be in my bunk until dark."

Far from hiding out, Rob kept tabs on the scene using his in-room periscope, which he'd asked De Vries to modify. Now it let him rotate the mirror system so he could see a short way in every direction. The hollow tubing also drew outdoor sound in. *Spying on the troops*, Rob thought, *is sometimes a necessary evil.* And one that paid off.

Rob heard guitar notes and a woman's voice and saw Gratiano stroll into view. He was with Rose, though, not Frida.

"Are you sure they'll all be at the cavalry training?" Rose asked.

The musician continued to pluck strings as he answered. "Attendance is mandatory. Er, compulsory. Definitely not optional. That is to say: they'll all be there."

Rob squinted into the periscope viewing window. His own words! Plus a few extra ones. Had Gratiano been eavesdropping on their meeting? Or had he found out about the order from Frida? And why would Rose want to know?

Just then, Frida and Turner appeared in range, and paired off with the other two. Gratiano plagued Frida with his flowery speech, while Rose rattled off a list of things that she wanted Turner to trade for.

The captain listened to the musician flatter Frida a moment, then turned his attention to the other partners. Rose's demands seemed in keeping with her job as interior designer: quartz and prismarine for tiles, glass for mirrors—and lots and lots of purple dye. When Rob thought it over, though, he realized that those materials could be crafting ingredients for more sophisticated items: redstone comparators, blast shields, beacons . . . and purple stuff.

"But, honey—it'll all have to wait till I get paid," Turner was saying to Rose.

"Well, when will that be?"

The sergeant hemmed and hawed. "Dunno. Seems I'm on probation just now. Why can't you just requisition those things from De Vries?"

Rose mentioned something about budget cuts and changed the subject.

Rob saw a party come in from the direction of town—one tall guy, one medium-built man in a cloak, one short woman swinging a pickaxe, and one giant head floating along. De Vries, Judge Tome, Crash, and Colonel M had arrived for drill practice. Turner took the opportunity to break away from Rose and sidle out of view. Rob could hear him handing out weapons and trying to get up another card game for later. Frida moved off to help Turner, and Rob saw Rose whisper something to Gratiano but couldn't make out her words.

A settler walked through periscope range placing night torches. Dusk was falling. Rob took off his vest and chaps, and exchanged them for a skin he'd grabbed from the Lost and Found. Then he left his watch post.

Time for action.

*

Rob picked his way along the vacant path to the city site. Settlers and workers had all gathered in the stands crafted next to the horse pasture to watch the troopers' mounted exercise. The south end of camp remained empty until a baby zombie spawned and wobbled toward the disguised captain. The rotting tot drew a wooden sword and faked a couple of lunges.

Unimpressed, Rob pulled a diamond pickaxe and lopped its oversized skull off with one stroke. "I don't have time for this," he growled, leaving the drops and hustling along. Instead of heading for the main gate, though, he stopped at the edge of the chainmail fence closest to camp. Then he cast a glance over his shoulder and hung a left, hurrying toward the rising cliffside.

At the spot where fence met cliff, Rob climbed a spruce tree, crawled his way to the edge of an overhanging limb, and swung down inside the compound. He paused a moment, listening, to make sure a guard hadn't seen him. Then he crept toward the entrance to the cavern that he and Crash had visited earlier. His mind whirled with details, possibilities, and contingencies—but behind them all was the mirthless laugh of the individual who was plotting against him.

Was it a man? Or was it some blend of human and animal with the power to destroy and move things, threaten and kill? Rob had been turning this idea over in his mind all day.

His flash of insight at the conference had taken him back to a long-ago afternoon on the ranch when he'd made an unwelcome discovery. He had stayed home from riding fences to work on the old barn, which needed mending. One of the big swinging doors had rotted away from its hinges—or so it seemed.

The cowboy had rounded up a hammer, nails, and an old board to use as a patch. But when he examined the door more closely, he found the wood degraded, not by moisture, but by a swarm of insects that had fed on the material. As he pushed the hinges aside, he heard a dull, rattling chirp—the sound a handful of jumping beans might make inside a paper bag. He peeled away a strip of paint that hung loose and, startled, recoiled.

Termites! The busy bugs were chewing on the barn door as Rob watched. He drew closer, fascinated. The creatures could actually live on cellulose and the other compounds in wood. They couldn't harm a medium-sized, relatively strong cowboy—but, left undisturbed, they could bring down an entire barn, eventually. Rob's patch wouldn't solve that problem.

He couldn't remember who had exterminated the pests, or how, and now he wished he could. While he'd never seen termites in this world, he had come across their cousins several times. It was likely that both types of insect had the same diet—and the same habit of unearthing gold deposits.

Silverfish! Could the arthropod mob be responsible for some of the mishaps on the build site? Rob was banking on it. If so, he'd be that much closer to identifying the sworn enemy of Beta, the battalion, and a free Overworld. Once he knew who—or what—he was dealing with, he could finally safeguard the pioneer population or call on his friends to help him do so. In any case, the next move would be his alone.

Rob lifted a wall torch and used it to light his way down the tunnel leading to the apartment complex. Soon he reached the honeycomb of holes that burrowed into the rock. *I doubt that a bunch of silverfish are plotting to destroy the Overworld union*, he reflected. *It's whoever is controlling them that I want to find.*

And whoever that was must have a base camp underground, or there would be a more obvious trail of evidence. What was it the crazed kidnapper had said? He was "perfectly comfortable" in Beta. So he must have somewhere to hide, and something to live on—resources of some kind.

Then Rob noticed a lump in the rock wall, a raised area in a square pattern. He felt it with his fingertips. It appeared to be a seam of some kind. He pressed his weight against the center of the square . . . and the wall slid silently backward, opening up a hole deep in the hillside.

"What the—?"

Cautiously, Rob moved forward, holding his torch high. The cave offshoot should have been a normal hollow in which ore veins and deposits would have collected. Clearly, it had been inhabited—by a man, if not a monster. A crafting table and furnace stood in one corner, surrounded by half-finished redstone circuitry and components. Across the stone room stood a huge stone closet. As Rob got closer to it, he recognized it as the dungeon his troopers had found on the day that the sinkhole had nearly swallowed up Frida.

Remembering what had happened to her, he carefully edged toward the door and peered inside, and saw the broken monster egg responsible for the silverfish. There were two chests. One of them lay open, and stacks of wheat and bread spilled from inside it. *That's what this griefer is living on!* Rob had to know what was in the other chest. To avoid any hidden pressure plates, he reached for the clasp from the side and flung it open.

The reflected light nearly blinded him, and he dropped his torch. He fell to his knees and groped for it, and then illuminated the contents of the chest again. It was full of gold! Gold ore, blocks, ingots, nuggets—even golden apples. Whoever this room belonged to had used the silverfish's natural attraction to the heavy metal to collect the stash. But why?

Rob got his answer when he returned to the crafting corner of the room. Some of the gold had been used to make weighted pressure plates, like the one he'd stepped on before. The UBO redstone stores had probably also contributed to the project. As he sorted through the pile of components and crafting ingredients, an ominous picture began to take shape. Gunpowder, redstone, pressure plates, trip wire . . . it looked as though someone were rigging a bomb.

Suddenly, a familiar rattle came from the other end of the tunnel. Rob froze, listening. It was the silverfish saying, *Honey, I'm home!*

*

Rob's days spent with Frida hadn't been for nothing. The survivalist was a master at blending in with her jungle surroundings. Her movements, her clothing, even her skin coloring all furthered her ability to travel undetected. This made her an excellent vanguard—a trooper who could lead out, preserving the element of surprise, or scout an enemy ambush before it could happen. After observing her in her native environment, Rob had learned that, in survival, knowing when to move and when to freeze made all the difference.

He knew those were his only choices now. If he waited until the silverfish got to his hiding place, he'd be toast. If he ran with them pursuing him, ditto. He snatched at the fleeting window of time between those two end points and skedaddled out of the bunker, unable to shut the hidden door in his haste. He streaked through the tunnel as fast as his boots would take him. Once outside, he dropped his torch in a water bucket and made for the fence line.

Like a live shadow, he retraced his steps to his entry point, only to find that the spruce limb was out of reach. He piled some blocks, conveniently discarded near the capitol foundation, to form steps. Then he managed to reach the tree, swing up, and make his getaway.

Back in camp, he had no choice but to remain in his bunk. His borrowed skin might be recognized by its owner, and his own clothing was in use right now. He put an eye to his periscope peephole, but he couldn't see all the way to the horse pasture, where the troopers were drilling. He gave up and went and slumped down in his easy chair.

Rob wouldn't be surprised to hear that another layer of the apartment tower had been eaten away that night. The silverfish's boss seemed to know when people would be nearby and when it was safe to work at destroying the city. Finding the mole might unlock the whole mystery.

A low knock at the door nearly caused Rob to cry out. Without waiting for an answer, the visitor pushed his way in. The man was about the captain's height and of a similar build—save for the bulbous head. This, of course, was only a jack-o'-lantern. Kim had borrowed Rob's mask to keep the man's identity a secret and to make people think he was the cavalry commander. The chaps and vest he wore completed the disguise. For an instant, Rob thought he was seeing himself in the mirror. Then he knew their ruse had worked.

"Swale, old man!"

The farmer removed his pumpkin head and stood there in Rob's signature duds, smiling. "I ain't never had so much fun," he admitted. Rob didn't know whether he meant the mounted drill or the subterfuge. "I hope it was some help to you."

"It was. How did Saber do for you?" Rob had known Swale could handle the stallion on the field and loaned him the horse to add credibility to his masquerade.

"Perfect. It's like he was in on the gag."

"And the training?"

"Just like you said. I had the troopers take turns calling the drill—for XP, we said—and I just followed along. Running in patterns, slashing at zombies . . . I do think I could make a cavalry soldier, someday."

Rob knew the adrenaline rush the farmer was enjoying. It was what incited men and women to embrace risk, danger, and death in the name of defending a cause. "Battalion Zero would be proud to have you, Swale . . . if you weren't so valuable on the horse farm. I hear that's some fine horse flesh you brought in today."

"Thank you kindly." He paused. "Well, I'd best be getting into my costume for the ride home." He swapped the vest and chaps for another item of leather clothing and balanced a pair of round-lensed sunglasses on his nose. "How do I look?"

The farmer posed in a black leather jumpsuit. Now Rob *could* see his own reflection in the sunglasses, and he smiled. "Like a Thunder Boy."

A few moments later, another signal knock came at the door. Kim had arrived, bent on pointing Swale toward a darkened section of minecart tracks. In that get-up, nobody would think twice about him leaving.

To complete the ploy, Rob put his own clothes plus the jack-o'-lantern mask back on and joined the crowd that was just breaking up at the pasture. He let the battalion cluster around him as he shook hands with spectators. The settlers had been impressed.

"Wonderful demo, Captain."

"Fine display of riding."

Rob nodded his pumpkin head, telling one woman the mask made him feel like just one of the troops when he had others play captain. "All the new recruits wear them," he explained.

"Well done, Private Rob," Stormie joked, in a tone of voice that said she hadn't been fooled.

"Troops!" Rob called. "Fall in for final inspection."

As the last of the crowd dispersed, Rob took advantage of his heavy mask to give his friends a quick recap of his activities—without anyone else being able to hear him or read his lips.

"I've discovered who is causing havoc in the city. It's a griefer, all right. With an army of minions, just like Lady Craven. But somebody is feeding this guy inside information. Someone who can get to us battalion members, the job offices, and probably the computer network, too. It's not safe to talk."

"Is it that Volt, sir?" Stormie guessed.

"Is it endermites, like Aswan said?" Kim pressed.

"Precisely, who *are* we dealing with?" Jools asked quietly.

Rob gave them a serious look through the eye holes of the jack-o'-lantern. "I don't know who, but I think I know what. I asked myself what could live underground, eat wood, and collect gold. While I believe it's silverfish doing the damage, someone is controlling them. It's their boss we're after."

Turner wanted a clear target. "Is it a man?"

"Maybe. But a man with the heart and mind of a tunneling insect."

Frida appeared disgusted by the prospect. With a fierce expression, she said, "Then let me squash him, sir."

*

Rob instructed the troopers to act as though they knew nothing about the source of the troubles in Beta. He hadn't mentioned being detained by someone who was intimidating potential biome delegates. He would have to pursue that lead himself, but he did ask his friends to keep their eyes and ears open for a mole.

"I should have known!" Jools lamented. "Moles live underground, too. And what better way to transmit information to other underworld scum than to use a mine as headquarters?"

"Frida, Turner," Rob said. "One more thing, before you leave for the flower forest: I want you to plant some bogus intel." He directed them to have a word with their significant others, being sure to say that a griefer's den had been discovered. "Oh, and tell Rose and Gratiano where you're going, and that it will take several days."

The vanguard and sergeant appeared uncertain of this tactic, but Stormie approved. "That should smoke out the mole, sir."

"Or at least rule out the innocent," Frida protested, and Turner nodded stubbornly.

"Okay, Bat Zero, this is it. Say no more until we find out who's leaking intel. And that had better be soon." Rob pictured the crafting area of the hidden room he'd found. If someone was building a bomb, exposing the mole couldn't happen soon enough.

CHAPTER 13

OW ROB DIDN'T DARE LEAVE THE VICINITY, and he hated to let Frida go. But she was right: someone had to interrogate the pumpkin farmer and work the truth out of her. She and Turner could perform a few more errands on their way south. With the sergeant at arms as backup, Frida would be as safe as she could be—on the trail, at night, in hostile territory.

It might not be any safer here in camp. Rob gave a long look toward his bed before turning in on the floor that night. He lay there, hoping he had made the right series of decisions. Leaking the silverfish plot was risky, but no one on the outside knew that it was the captain who had located the mob boss's underground lair. Anyone could have done it. Leaving that bunker door open might turn out to be a happy accident.

Rob was fairly certain he was on track in baiting Rose and Gratiano. They had been awfully chummy lately, and one or the other—or both—of them could be part of the intelligence network. They had certainly put themselves in places that made them privy to details. For once, it wasn't the candid cowboy whose loose tongue had caused the battalion grief.

Rob rolled over and sighed. It just went to show that dabbling in romance could be more dangerous than an honest fight. But, even his survivalist friends, who should know better, sometimes gave in to the need for human companionship. As a veteran range rider, though, the captain knew how to get the next-best thing.

He couldn't sleep, so he got dressed and slipped out of the bunkhouse. The horses mumbled under their breaths as he quietly lowered the drawbridge and let himself into the pasture. First Saber, and then Redstone, drifted up to greet him. The two horses battled for his attention, so Rob ended up simultaneously scratching their shoulders, saying nothing, using only their language to communicate.

Soon Redstone's head drooped, and she lowered herself on folded legs to snooze some more. But Saber seemed to sense the captain's need for camaraderie. He stood staunchly by Rob's side, even when the scratching stopped. The night sky was shrouded in low clouds, leaving only Saber's hind white socks clearly visible.

Then Rob sensed movement outside the pasture fence, and the horses began stirring. He heard a low growl, followed by a short, quick, piercing cry—and then silence. Something other than grazing animals was feeding out here. Rob stuck with Saber as the horse gave a few quick turns, following the stallion's ears to the source of the commotion.

The filmy clouds pulled apart, leaving enough moonlight to reveal two four-legged creatures running through the grass. *They're coming this way!* Rob took his cue from Saber, whose muscles had coiled but who stood his ground. When the pair of animals was nearly at the pasture boundary, Rob made out a familiar diamond marking on their heads. These wolves were friendly. Saber's keen sense of smell told him so, too.

"*Psst!*" Rob called to the visitors once Saber had relaxed and given the rest of the horses the all-clear.

The canines raised their heads, stopped, and then resumed a slower approach. They halted just on the other side of the moat and fence. Before Rob's eyes, their forms began to quiver. They lost definition, hovering somewhere between wolf and shapelessness. Then their outlines grew taller, more definite . . . and more human.

As the two players donned their respective skins, Rob greeted them in a low voice. "Crash. De Vries. What are you two doing out here?"

The miner pulled her pickaxe from her inventory and pretended it was a bow, which she loaded with a make-believe arrow.

"Hunting, eh?"

De Vries nodded and whispered, "We didn't want to freak anyone out."

The rare shape shifters might easily have frightened a settler into sounding an alarm or taking up arms. Their wolf forms had benefited the battalion in the past, but also put the brother and sister at risk of retaliation by superstitious or ignorant people. Seeing them now made Rob realize that he had missed a valuable surveillance opportunity.

With the building and mining past their busy stages, Rob felt he could ask another favor of the pair. He couldn't share all the specifics, but he could put their alternate skins to good use. "Why not patrol the build site at night for us? I've got a line on a possible mole but don't want to scare it off. We need a guard that will allow our troopers covert access to the mines."

Crash licked her lips. It seemed that only live prey satisfied her wolf side, and she'd be glad of the chance to nab the odd small animal.

"I'm tired of sleeping, anyway," De Vries said. "When should we start?"

Rob thought about it, absently petting Saber. "Let me announce it tomorrow. If innocent folks know wolves are roaming, they'll stay away—and griefers won't mind what they say around you, or suspect you of protecting us."

Satisfied, they went their separate ways.

*

As Rob had predicted, Rose Manor lost another floor overnight. He set the builder—in his human form—to the task of raising the apartment towers and replacing their wooden foundations with cobblestone. Rob wanted no more delays between now and the city's move-in and inauguration dates. They were literally in a race against time. While the captain could not yet divulge that someone was crafting a time bomb, he felt every second ticking away.

So, forced to wait anxiously for Turner's and Frida's return, he passed the time by helping the construction crew lift the high-rise buildings and poke shims underneath. De Vries was in his prime human element supervising the momentous labor.

Whole spruce trees had been moved downhill and "planted" in the ground around the apartment

buildings to act as sturdy cranes. These were equipped
with wooden pulleys that Crash crafted from Rat's old
cart wheels, and those were slung with seemingly miles
of spider-string ropes. The rope nets were draped over
the wooden towers to enable hoisting from the ground.
Rob joined the volunteer army of settlers that grabbed
ropes, stretched them taut, and waited for the signal
from De Vries.

The builder had made his calculations, pitting
weight and force against height and gravity's resis-
tance. He'd checked the day's temperature, humidity,
and wind speed. He'd considered the number of workers and their physical capabilities, and even inquired
what they'd had to eat that morning. Every base covered, he gave the order: "Three . . . two . . . one: *pull!*
Pull! Put your backs into it!"

Rob and dozens more men and women tugged,
letting their weight do most of the work. At first,
nothing seemed to happen. Then, little by little, the
buildings began to move. They rose like a logging
operation in reverse—trees going up instead of being
sawn through and knocked down. Rob could only see
directly in front of him, but could sense the towers
rising as one.

"Shim crew: *now!*" cried De Vries, and then, a
moment later, "Rope crew: *halt!*" Next, he urged
them to gently—ever so gently—relax their holds and

let the weight of the buildings settle the ropes and, finally, the structures themselves.

An enormous cheer went up from the spectators. When the crews were released, Rob and the others stumbled backward to view their handiwork. There sat the three towers, neat as huge wooden pins, sitting on cross-logs to await their new foundations. That work would be done just a swiftly, with Crash over-seeing the stone stacking. The settlers were one step closer to home.

"Congratulations, sir!" Stormie praised the cap-tain's effort.

"Same to you, Artilleryman." She had served on the shim crew. "But don't thank me yet. Removing this temptation is only part of our job," he said more quietly.

"Well, then, I take it back: un-congratulations. Until further notice." She grinned. "Good to be work-ing with you again, anyway. What's next?"

Rob could always count on the adventurer to be watching the horizon. "The settlers' lodgings are nearly secure. I guess it's time to see whether our mole has taken the bait. Let's find Jools and Kim, then dial Aswan."

Jools and Kim were already in the conference room, working on a web page for Beta. "Someday I imagine this place will be quite the tourist magnet," Jools said.

Kim put a fist to her chin. "We need a catchy tag line. Like . . . *Beta: Best of All Biomes*."

Jools thought it over. "Or, how about *Beta: Making Overworld History Daily*? You like to travel, Stormie. What d'you think?"

"Quartermaster, another time," Rob interrupted. "Get Aswan onscreen. Let's see if he's learned what we told our . . . friends." At this point, Jools's personal online connection seemed more secure than the one set up for the city network.

Shortly, his computer screen showed the leather worker's lively face. "I was just about to contact you, Captain! Following the previous communication route, I intercepted another exchange late last night."

"You're working overtime, Delegate."

"My ears never sleep," Aswan said, flashing several gold teeth.

His intel was not news to the assembled battalion members. Aswan repeated what he'd heard: that two of their cavalry mates had ridden out of Beta to the south at midnight. They were bound for "an alliance contact" in the flower forest and would return in a few days.

"It would appear that somebody wants to know when Battalion Zero is together as a unit," Jools interpreted. "Or, when the city's guard is at less than full strength."

"And the source, Aswan?" Rob asked.

"Same as before: in or very near Beta. That's as close as I can get."

"If you get any closer on anything, let us know." Rob motioned for Jools to sign off.

Again, they were immediately summoned by Gaia. Jools connected, and this time, the genial priest looked alarmed. "I fear that something big is coming your way," she warned. "Someone has extended the Spike City rail tracks off to the east. We received a report from trappers coming from cold beach. They followed the minecart tracks to see where they went, and they just . . . end. At the ocean." She transmitted images that the trappers had captured as proof.

This stunned the four troopers. "And no one saw this extra track being laid?" Rob asked.

"No. Before they took the job with you, my boys replaced the rails and capped off the ends at our village. We woke up the other day to find they'd been tampered with."

Rob spoke to Jools. "There's no way the Thunder Boys could've done this, is there?"

The quartermaster shook his head. "Believe me, I've made it my life's work to keep them busy. I'll vouch for them."

Rob turned back to Gaia. "Don't touch those tracks. I'll tell you if I learn anything more. And Delegate . . . we appreciate the support."

"You have it, Captain."

At least they hadn't lost any UBO affiliates. But they still had to gain some. Rob told Jools, Kim, and Stormie to prepare for a trail ride whenever Frida and Turner got back from their mission.

*

Rob practically counted the seconds until their return. He acted so jittery that Kim asked him to work with her and Redstone to help him forget his worries, at least for a little while. The shiny red filly found everything they asked her to do new and exciting. Seeing her decide to cross a scary box full of rocks reminded the cowboy of his old life and the pony he'd been training when his vacation had suddenly been extended.

"You and I should go into business together," Kim said, half-joking. "They say you should work at what you love."

Rob regarded the filly, which was playfully nosing around an old spider eye. "Well, it's nice to know I'll have a job waiting for me when my enlistment is up."

The absorbing activity helped fill the hours until, late one afternoon, the absent troopers rode in. Rob made sure he was there to meet them, and he made a big enough fuss to alert everyone in camp to their return. So, Kim, Stormie, Jools—and Rose and Gratiano—were there to welcome Turner and Frida, too.

"Sorry to let you rest only briefly, troopers," Rob said. "We'll be leaving again on a trail ride just after mess call."

This interested Rose, who had attached herself to Turner's arm. "A moonlight ride? How romantic! Can I go with you, Turnie? Can I? Gratiano could come along and strum for us."

"But . . . you don't ride, sweetums. Fact is, you told me horses smell like poop, and they bite."

"They probably just bite *you*," Stormie muttered.

"Sorry, no civilians," Rob said, ending the debate. "Company business."

"What *kind* of business?" Rose switched her tractor-beam gaze on him.

Stormie reached out and took Rose's chin firmly in her hand and turned her head away. "*Private* company business," she said, avoiding eye contact.

"Or as private as zombie killing can be," Rob added. "We'll be back before daylight . . . or whenever the zombies give out."

Stymied, Rose stood there tapping a purple-heeled foot after the troopers moved off. She had no choice but to stay behind, along with Gratiano and anyone else who didn't want to make a show of pursuing them.

After dinner, the six horse soldiers mounted up and rode out of civilian earshot for a debriefing. Rob ordered Stormie to lead them west, away from the grounds of their skeleton hunt—and Rob's encounter with the mob boss. When they reached a suitable spot, the captain called for a horse huddle, and the debriefing began.

First, he and Jools described the conversations with Aswan and Gaia. Aswan's latest message pointed to Rose or Gratiano being either the griefer spy or reporting to an unidentified one. This meant that one or both of the settlers were untrustworthy.

Frida took this news with silent acceptance. Turner did not.

"There ain't a dishonest bone in that woman's body!" he argued.

Jools snorted. "Let's see. How many men does Rose have catering to her whims right now?" He pretended to run out of fingers, counting.

Stormie brought up Rose's demanding attitude. "How come she wants so much? First a job, then a penthouse . . ."

Rob murmured, ". . . and some suspicious crafting ingredients." He looked at Turner. "I hate to break this to you, Sergeant, but she's been playing you. Where I come from—"

"Hey! Spare me your conspiracy theories, Newbie. Ya can't con a con man. If there's a mole out there, it ain't Rose." He folded his arms decisively. "And, guess what: nobody knows where they come from. That 'world' of yours? Mebbe it ain't there at all. Could be you've been in this game from the get-go."

This shocked Rob into silence.

"Don't listen to him, Captain," Stormie said quietly. "He's just yankin' your chain."

"Everybody's got a past," Kim asserted.

"Yeah, but not everybody's got a future," Turner spit out. "Leastways, not here. I ain't gettin' paid for this." He picked up the reins, spun Duff around, and took off for camp.

Frida backed Ocelot up, at the ready.

"Let him go, Corporal," Rob said. "He can't get in any deeper than he already is."

After an awkward moment, Rob asked Frida how their trip had gone.

"Not so hot on the shakedown," she admitted. "Our farmer friend can't be in the top tier of any alliance. She has pieces of info but not the whole puzzle. Don't worry, though, Captain. We questioned her in such a way that she didn't learn anything from us."

"Good," Rob said.

"Not good," Jools countered. "That means we're stuck where we were before. This Volt person could be working for Lady Craven or Bluedog, or could be a lone opportunist."

"Doesn't matter," Stormie pointed out. "We know one of the bigs is targeting Beta. Even if Volt is carrying information to them from our mole, the result is the same."

"Exactly," Kim agreed. "They basically know where we live. We're a target—and either the Griefer Imperial Army or some other gang is coming for us."

"Isn't that what we wanted, Captain?" Frida said. "It's why we quit running. To give Lady Craven and her types a bull's-eye, instead of us chasing them all over. Right?"

"Right. Well, it is, and it isn't." Rob rubbed his eyes wearily. "We didn't expect to have a city full of people here when they attacked us."

Now that the mole or moles had been exposed, the captain could tell his troopers how grave the situation was. He recounted his episode with the mob boss and what he'd found in his subterranean "nest."

"Those do sound like the makings for a bomb," Stormie said worriedly. "Do you think he'll use it to upset Beta's grand opening?"

Kim did. "A bomb at a public ribbon-cutting would send a loud message to the rest of the biomes."

"But all is not lost," Rob said. "The good news is, if we can defuse that little problem, we are on the cusp of a new, unified Overworld."

"How so?"

"Frida?" Rob prompted.

"The captain asked Turner and me to make a few pit stops on our way back. We managed to sign the next six northern biomes . . . although several villagers mentioned Volt's name—they said he'd threatened to burn their towns if they voted with the UBO. But, their delegates are strong. They claim the people are a hundred percent for unification."

"Even with the intimidation?" a skeptical Jools asked.

Frida nodded. "Because of it."

"But now Rose will find out about your biome outreach," Kim said.

"Yes, Turner's not known for his tact," Jools observed.

"That's okay," Rob said. "We *want* her to find out about it. She'll report back to the boss, forcing him to act prematurely. We can't really do anything until he comes out in the open."

"And we'll be ready for him," Stormie said.

"We will be ready. The Beta celebration and ribbon-cutting will go on as planned. This will draw whatever fire is planned for us." Rob looked at Frida. "Vanguard, I want you to relay the news about the city inauguration to Gratiano. Unless I miss my guess, he'll forward it to the head honcho."

Frida considered the request to rat out her sweet-heart. Then she said, "Seems like we all have to put something on the line if we want to win this battle."

Rob could see that she'd been hurt. Misplacing trust was a mistake the survivalist did not take lightly. But denial was not her style.

"Okay, sir," she said. "I'll do it."

CHAPTER 14

WHEN THE SPLINTERED BATTALION GOT BACK to cavalry camp, Frida went to find Gratiano and plant the information that would set their fate in motion. But she came back to the bunkhouse having been unable to locate him.

"It's late," Rob said. "Where is he?"

"I can tell ya that." Turner entered the room and plopped down in a chair next to the furnace. "Rose's penthouse." He blew out a heavy breath. "They run off together."

Rob noticed the uncommonly dejected expression on the sergeant's face. He knew that look—and that feeling. They were the same ones he'd witnessed when some cowboy got thrown from a bronc—or when he did.

"That stinks!" Kim cried. "Using sweetness as a weapon."

"Or, in Rose's case, a reasonable facsimile of sweetness," Jools said.

Turner was feeling sorry for himself again. "I don't mind tellin' ya, I'm . . . real sad. I believed in that woman."

"Which is just what she wanted," Stormie said darkly.

Frida reached over and put a hand on Turner's mountain biome tattoo. "Don't worry about it, Meat. I got hit, too."

"Yeah, well. I notice you ain't cryin'."

"That's because I've got a better idea." She gave him a wicked grin. "Don't get sad; get mad."

"You mean, fight back?"

"Best thing we can do is take the big boss down."

This rocked him out of his wallow. He looked at her a moment, then made up his mind. "Amen, sister. Amen."

The captain smiled to himself, thinking that Colonel M would be proud of this outcome. Rob should have known that his troopers would rise to the occasion. When Frida and Turner got mad, there was no stopping them. To them, *anger management* involved an arsenal of weapons and a visit to their enemies. Letting them mow down any griefers in their path would simply be allowing nature to take its course.

"Count me in!" said Kim, eager to defend her friends' honor.

Again, Rob would have to defer to his trooper's natural talents. He was through worrying when this griefer would strike. It was time to invite a battle.

Rob crafted some lengths of paper and asked Stormie for her brushes and dyes. Then he made up some banners, which read:

BETA CITY CELEBRASHUN
Celebriddy Appearanses
Ribbon Cutting
Perade – Games – Firewerks
TWO DAYS ONLY
STARTS TOMORROW AT DUSK

"How does that look?" he asked Jools when he finished three identical signs.

Jools quickly scanned them. "Well . . . you spelled *dusk* correctly."

This was good enough for the captain.

"Shall I have some of the village children hang them?"

"Yes. We've got plenty to do before then. Stormie, announce to the settlers that move-in day will take place after the party and inauguration. That'll keep them safely in camp watching the fireworks while we root out the city's . . . infestation. Then the judge and colonel will be in the clear for ribbon-cutting the next day. Oh, and Stormie, get to work on your boom-booms, too. We'll want some live rounds in addition to the fireworks."

"Ten-four, Captain."

"Jools," Rob continued. "Run those images of the new minecart track by the Thunder Boys. See if they have any clues. We've got to be able to fend off whatever might be coming our way from that end before we go underground. And we'll need some enchantments to boost our kill power."

"On it," the quartermaster acknowledged.

"Kim, get some help washing and grooming horses for the parade . . . and putting up decorations. Even if the event is a front for our counterattack, we do want to make a good impression for the UBO."

The horse master nodded. "I've been crafting fancy saddle blankets with a city crest on them. We can hang matching bunting on the main street."

"You'll be in charge of diverting attention, then. Can you put on one of your circus acts with the horses before the fireworks?"

"You bet. I'll add in some audience participation. Everybody'll be on the edge of their seats."

"Right on." Now Rob relayed his most daring part of the plan. "Frida, Turner. We need to find out where the silverfish are holing up and exterminate them."

Frida stared at him in disbelief. "You know that silverfish and I . . . don't get along."

"That's exactly why I've chosen you for the job. No one hates those bugs as much as you do." She couldn't argue with that. "De Vries and Crash will be patrolling the site as wolves after hours. They'll let us in." He pushed back from the dining table. "Let's get word to the judge and colonel to get their ribbon-cutting program together. If we're to have the proper cover, this 'party' has got to look authentic."

The captain wanted to bring up the subject of spawn points once more, but he couldn't very well ask for what he hadn't yet done himself. There was still time, though.

"And, battalion." Rob put his hands on the table and leaned over for a final word. "Put your free time to good use. I want every sword in our inventory sharpened, enchanted, and ready to go by tonight."

*

The city began to take on a festive air with banners, flags, and flowers hung for all to see. The repaired high-rise buildings awaited their first inhabitants. The capitol complex, now about three-quarters complete, was gaining personality. Decorative steps, pillars, and De Vries's intricately cut windows distinguished the main building as a seat of government.

Back in camp, booths for food and game vendors had been set up. Stormie and Kim were doing a good job of drawing attention to the celebration itinerary, which Rob knew would filter through Rose and Gratiano to the proper griefer contacts. Jools had the Thunder Boys analyzing the minecart rail system to try to determine what sort of outside threat might be in the works. Rob met with Judge Tome and Colonel M to see if he'd neglected anything.

He found them together, practicing their speeches in the conference room.

"Have you neutralized our moles yet?" the judge asked.

Rob shook his head. "They're unaware that we know their identities, so they might still be valuable to us."

"That is a point in your favor," Colonel M said. "You are wise to play them for their usefulness rather than to seek revenge."

Rob gave a wry smile. "I can't guarantee how long that'll last. My troopers want them to pay for their deception."

The colonel rolled his head in acknowledgement. "Rose and Gratiano still have the ear of your target.

Perhaps threatening their lives will help you identify this griefer and reveal his motives, once and for all."

"You mean torture?"

"That would be against the Overworld's articles of war," Judge Tome counseled. "Besides, sophisticated means of extracting information would be wasted on those *tabulae rasae.*"

Colonel M agreed. "They are a couple of clean slates. Once you get past their overconfident facades, they really are quite simple underneath."

"What do you suggest then?"

Colonel M chuckled. "Scare them."

Rob thought this advice over. He could give the two moles what they deserved and throw their boss off track long enough to get in and out of the mines safely. If he accomplished that, the battalion would be well situated to put a swift end to the griefer plot.

He asked Jools to have the Thunder Boys program a minecart and station it at the city gate. Then he rounded up Frida and Turner. "I have another job for you. I think you'll enjoy it."

Rose's decorating contract had not yet been cancelled. She had taken to working from her posh penthouse, and Gratiano was now playing go-fer. Frida and Turner would be able to use him to get to her. The two survivalists waited and watched the entrance to ROSE 1 from a blind they made in the farm's growing pumpkin patch. Then they saw the opportunity they were waiting for.

As the corrupt musician carried an armload of wool rugs into the high-rise, they left the blind and trailed him at a discreet distance. Silently, they followed him upstairs to the top floor. He balanced the bulky load and fumbled for the door.

"About time!" snapped Rose as he entered. "I've been waiting."

"Begging your pardon, my rose petal. I do apologize. Please forgive me," Gratiano said. "It won't happen again."

"You're darn tootin' it won't," Turner said ominously. He and Frida slipped inside. She slammed the door shut behind them, and Turner pulled his diamond axes from their shoulder holsters.

The two unarmed players stared at them.

"Thought you could throw me over for another man, did you?" Turner accused Rose.

Frida drew the special double-bladed sword that the battalion had commissioned for her after their last campaign—diamond on one side and gold on the other. She flew across the room and planted it at Gratiano's jugular vein. "You weren't in love with me. You were planning all along to use me up and throw me out like last night's trash."

"I-I was well paid for it," Gratiano blustered. "I was low on gems. I needed the money. You wouldn't fault a man for trying to make a living, would you?"

Frida snarled and shoved her blade against his neck. "Dying ain't much of a living, boy."

"And you," Turner snapped at Rose. "How much was you gettin' to make me out the fool?"

She raised her hands in the air, giving him a rancid look. "Not enough, it seems."

"Well, it's payback time now. He flipped his axes through the air. *P-lack! Th-wack!* The blades sliced through the sleeves of her purple blouse and pinned her skin to the paneled wall.

Her bravado melted away. "Wh-what are you going to do with us?"

"I'ma send you two on a little vacation," Turner said with false charm in his voice.

"Somewhere you won't be coming back from any-time soon," Frida added. "But first, Gratiano, I think you need a little *haircut.*" Her blade flashed, removing a hunk of his cascading locks and returning to his throat.

"That's right," Turner said, securing a block of TNT from his inventory. "Let me help you two get *packed.*" He tossed it in the air and caught it. Then he clicked on it with some flint and steel. "There. It's primed. It'll make your minecart journey a real guessin' game."

"M-minecart?" Gratiano echoed.

"I hear the ocean is lovely this time of year," Frida said grimly.

The immobilized Rose realized the vanguard was talking about using the newly laid tracks. "You wouldn't run us out of town on a rail. . . ."

"Wouldn't we?" Turner stood in front of her, casually tossing the TNT block from hand to hand.

"Wait! I have information!"

Gratiano whimpered, "W-we can tell you what's coming in on those tracks."

The threats shook loose the news that the griefer army was planning to load enchanted mobs in mine-carts and unleash them on the city, when the celebration was in full swing.

"Who's behind it?" Frida demanded, turning her blade over against Gratiano's neck.

The musician squirmed. "We—don't know!"

"Then you've just bought yourselves a one-way ticket!" Frida cocked her head at Turner.

He reached for one of the axes that pinned Rose to the wall and freed it, menacing her with it.

She caved. "No . . . wait! All we know is who we're supposed to report to. We've never even met him. He's the one in charge of the mobs. He'd kill us if he knew we'd said anything."

"A name?" Frida demanded.

All Rose would say was, "He's one of the GIA operatives."

Turner used the razor-sharp diamond blade to slice off one of her false purple eyelashes.

"Okay! Okay! The only thing I know is, he's called... Termite."

Turner and Frida exchanged glances. Then Turner set down the block of TNT and removed the other axe from the wall. Before Rose could stir, he wrapped both tattooed arms around her and, as she struggled, threw her down on one of the new rugs and rolled her up in it.

Frida took advantage of Gratiano's surprise to give him the same treatment. The two players kicked and screamed, but Turner and Frida held them tightly in the woolen wraps.

"Hey!" Rose yelled. "You promised to let us go!"

"No, I didn't," Turner said.

"It was implied," Gratiano argued. "Inferred, anyway. You certainly gave us a great, big hint—"

Frida knocked him in the head with the butt of her sword. "You talk too much," she said to the unconscious man.

Rose blinked at her captors through the rolled-up end of rug.

"You got somethin' to say, too?" Turner dared her. She did not.

"That's what I thought." He wrapped some spider string around the two human bundles. "C'mon, Corporal," he said. "Let's get 'em out of here."

*

The two helpless spies were placed in the waiting minecart along with the block of TNT and sent off up the hill. One of the Steves had programmed the vehicle for a nonstop trip to the end of the line. As far as the troopers were concerned, the snitches deserved to meet the very mobs they'd been paid to attract.

Their misfortune helped considerably to heal Turner's wounds. "Every time a woman weasels out on me, turns out she's doin' me a favor," he said with satisfaction. The troopers now knew the purpose of the new length of railway plus the name of the griefer who had infiltrated Beta city.

"I guess clouds do have golden linings," Frida mused.

The jilted troopers reported the success of their mission to the captain and the rest of the battalion as they gathered in the common room for dinner.

When Rob heard the griefer's name, he exclaimed, "*Termite?* So Aswan got half of the name right. It's perfect for that insect."

"What's a termite?" Frida asked.

Jools explained its close relationship to silverfish, which made her grimace. "But, don't worry, Corporal. Termites are extinct in the Overworld."

Pleased, Rob said he'd add an emerald bonus to each of the survivalists' paychecks—which they could claim whenever they met the battalion's . . . requirement.

Turner gave Rob a long look. "You sure you'll be there to pay up once this is over?" he challenged.

"I promise," Rob said, choking a little. "So, the only remaining questions are, who put this Termite on our tails? Who ordered the mob hit? And who is it that's trying to bring down a unified Overworld?"

Jools pounded the dining table. "Don't you see? The M.O. points squarely to Lady Craven. Consorting with vermin. Enchanting zombies. Dividing and conquering. It's got to be her."

Kim threw down her chicken leg. "And she's hiding behind layers of griefer scum."

"Maybe her new HQ *is* somewhere out in the ocean," Stormie said. "What with the tracks headin' off that way."

Kim drew her pink sword. "You want us to go after her, Captain?"

Stormie clenched a fist. "I'm with Kim."

Rob couldn't help but be amused by the horse master's quick temper and Stormie's determination when it came to rooting out injustice in the world. "First things first," he said. "We need to take down Termite."

"Maybe that'll put an end to this," Jools added.

Stormie glared at him. "Doin' right ain't got no end."

"She has a point," Rob agreed.

"That's square with me," said Turner. "Leads to steady work."

"But you've made most of your money by working for the other side," Jools mentioned.

"I like to keep my options open."

"Then tell us, Sergeant," Rob broke in. "What're our options for tonight? We'll need enough firepower to blast our way through a mountainside while avoiding setting off a bomb and being overrun by swarms of potentially enchanted silverfish. Meanwhile, we'll hafta keep the horses and settlers from being slaughtered and all of De Vries's and Crash's hard work from being destroyed."

If Rob expected this brainteaser to silence the egotistical mercenary, he was dead wrong. "Glad you asked, Captain," Turner said. "I been thinking things over. Here's what we'll do. . . ."

CHAPTER 15

A MESSAGE FROM GAIA ARRIVED AFTER DINNER informing Battalion Zero that the spy-laden minecart had passed Spike City on its way east. "By the time you get this video," she said, "any griefers on the other end will have found them."

"That'll make Lady Craven madder than a stuck pig," Stormie said to her cavalry mates.

"That means she'll be sending the mobs this way!" Kim cried.

"Just as we planned," Rob reminded her. "If our moles were telling the truth, Termite will have to meet them. That'll give us a chance to get inside his nest, trap the silverfish, and figure out how to disarm the bomb."

"Are you sure you can stop Termite from doing his job?" Frida asked. "He'd likely target our horses and the pioneers' tent camp before coming to polish us off. Then there'd be nobody to stop the bombing."

Jools crossed his arms. "Leave that to Turner and me. It's all taken care of."

"Then let's win this," Rob said with finality.

The cavalry commander hoped Turner's scheme was sound. There would be no time for sleep or spawn-point reassigning before tonight's invasion of the cavern. But as soon as they took care of the silverfish, Rob intended to make good on his promise to Turner—just in time for the city's inauguration. The cowboy-turned-cavalry commander might be from another world, but he owed his allegiance to this one.

*

The sunset that evening was spectacular. Rob hoped his strategy would be, too. As gold, pink, and orange rays deepened into shades of purple-gray, Battalion Zero went into action. Jools, Kim, and Stormie stayed behind in cavalry camp to play their roles while Rob, Frida, and Turner headed for the city's caverns.

The twin iron golems let them pass through the chainmail fence, and two alert wolves with black diamonds on their foreheads escorted them to the construction site. Rob felt an eerie sensation as they approached the cliffside. This place had seen so many of his victories and defeats. It was almost as though it were a player, itself—or someone behind the game, writing software that could change lives.

Turner must have felt it, too. "Believe I've had enough of the extreme hills for a while," he remarked.

"Yeah, Meat?" Frida said. "What're you gonna do when this is all over?"

"Let's see, now. First thing, I'll draw my pay and get me a stack o' steaks. Then, light out under cover of night and take a nice, long holiday. Somewhere . . . quiet."

"Unless another job comes up," she teased.

"Well, a lucrative one—sure."

She knew the man well.

Near the entrance to the caves, De Vries and Crash let out little whines. The troopers would wait there, hidden by stacked blocks, until the wolves barked, signalling when they saw Termite leave.

Rob and company settled into silence.

The captain tried to push all thoughts from his mind, wishing his heartbeat would ease up, but he couldn't help wondering what Frida was thinking. She had an amazing capacity to focus and put survival first, herself second. *I'm probably way down her list.* When this mission ended, Rob swore he'd change that.

Three sharp *yip*s bounced off the cliff wall, then a huddled human form scurried by.

"I could take him out now," Frida offered in a low voice.

"Stick to the script," Turner scolded and emerged from the hiding spot.

Rob said nothing and followed them into the cave—and into total blackness. Crash had already extinguished all the torches.

Too many lights would scare off the silverfish, so the group relied on Turner's "borrowed" mining cap to cut through the dark. Rob and Frida kept their swords drawn and, without breaking stride, quickly dispatched the zombies and skeletons that spawned in the gloom.

Rob directed Turner down the tunnel toward the silverfishes' honeycomb hideout. "Okay. Set out the bait."

Turner emptied his inventory of stacked sticks beneath the wall riddled with tiny holes.

"Now, let's lure 'em in." Rob picked up a stick and started gnawing on it loudly. He motioned for the others to start chewing, as well.

Frida hesitated, clearly icked out by the idea of asking the silverfish for a meeting, on purpose.

"That's an order," Rob said, and she reluctantly chose a stick and did as he asked.

Soon, a muffled chittering flowed through the tiny cave shafts. The sound made by scuttling arthropods made Rob flash on that barn-mending day on the ranch, and on how his memory of the termite nest had led to his conclusion about the silverfish. It seemed odd that insects would cause his two worlds to collide.

The noise grew louder. The mobsters were nearing the ends of the tunnels. Goosebumps rose on Rob's skin as he and Turner exchanged their wooden lures for swords. Frida dropped her stick and froze.

Rob saw her go catatonic, like a parachuter who'd lost her nerve and needed a push. "Corporal!" Rob said harshly. "Don't be a wimp. You've got two choices now: you can live, or you can die."

There was a suspenseful pause; then Rob saw anger light up Frida's face. She snapped out of her reverie and leaned into him, growling, "Don't you *ever* call me a wimp . . . sir!" Then she drew her favorite sword and a gold axe, and called into the tunnels: "C'mon out, now. It's suppertime!"

Turner added quietly, "And you're the main course."

Right on cue, the silverfish spilled out of the wall.

Jools had finally broken his bottle o' enchanting and used his increased XP level toward bane of arthropod enchantments for the battalion swords. Using them would slow the bugs' movements and deal them greater damage than usual. Even if the swords broke or the troopers pulled another weapon, the spell would still work—as long as they held the enchanted sword while they hit the silverfish.

Frida appreciated this edge. As it turned out, she also appreciated the cave's transportation system: the tiny tunnels acted as candy dispensers, spitting out arthropods like gumballs. Here they came, one after another, as though asking to be instantly sliced, diced, or impaled.

T-ing! T-oing! TONG! Frida's short and long blades accommodated all sizes of silverfish. Each stroke dealt a death blow. Her sword arm became a guillotine. As her technique became mechanically efficient, she called, "I'm starting to like shopping in bulk like this, guys!"

Turner was enjoying the kill rhythm, as well. "Big discounts, large *economy* size!" he barked, swinging his enchanted sword like a sickle of death.

Rob recalled his earlier target practice with the insects and employed the skewering technique, grateful that he had sharpened his blade well.

The troopers' skirmishing skill rivaled the bugs' prolific spawning ability. The three soldiers worked so quickly that piles of dead silverfish stacked up before they could disappear, until they nearly reached the outlet holes.

"Hey!" Rob yelled. "Maybe we can suffocate the rest of 'em in there!"

Frida considered but dismissed the notion. "No way. We can't risk it! If there's an exit at the other end, it won't work."

"Cover me," Turner said, and he left his stream of prey to scoop the dead insects away. Then he resumed the melee.

Time passed. Bodies accumulated and disintegrated. Still, the silverfish kept coming.

"They must've heard about my manly allure," Turner said, amazed at their numbers.

"Maybe they heard about the cavalry and wanted to enlist," Rob offered.

The metronomic slice of Frida's blade began to slow. Rob and Turner had to stab at a few mobsters that made it through her gauntlet. "I don't know how much longer I can keep this up!" she admitted.

Her health began to diminish. Then Rob and Turner started to lose hearts, and silverfish began to slip past them.

"Captain!" Turner called. "This might be one o' those times to fall back and regroup!"

They'd have to retreat to safety. "Give me your cap, Turner!" The sergeant tossed him the lighted helmet, and he jammed it on his head. "To the bunker!" Rob motioned for the other two to cut and run after him.

They dashed for the secret chamber in the rock, which was, fortunately, not too far down the cave corridor. On came the arthropods, some of them slowed by glancing blows, others scurrying to catch the players.

On the verge of panic, Rob felt for the seams in the wall and heaved himself against the spot. He stumbled inside, then quickly gave his friends cover as they spilled through the door with silverfish at their feet. Turner managed to replace the secret stone, and Frida helped Rob slay the remaining attackers.

Then all was silent.

When she dared to speak again, Frida said, "I could swear we've been through this before."

Rob wiped a few stray legs and antennae off his enchanted blade. "I guess that's why you're so good at it."

Frida shivered in disgust. "This is one skill I wish I didn't have."

Turner nodded. "I wish killin' silverfish was more like fishin'."

"Well, cowpokes," Rob said, "if wishes were cattle we'd all be eating hamburger."

*

When they had rested for a few moments, Rob pulled some torches out of his inventory and lit the room. He switched off his headlamp.

"Now . . . let's find out what our friend Termite is crafting."

In the corner of the chamber stood the furnace and crafting table, and a few discarded sticks. But the pile of incendiary materials Rob had seen before was gone.

"That stuff was right—here. . . ."

Turner squinted.

"Maybe someone moved it?" Frida suggested.

This possibility sent a wave of misery through the group. How would they search for the bomb without a clue?

"Maybe the dungeon has some evidence!"

"Let me, sir." Frida insisted on scouting it out first, even after what had happened the last time.

She approached the square stone enclosure and entered it . . . and a few seconds later, she backed out.

Rob asked, "All clear—?" Then he saw another player advance, holding an iron sword level with Frida's heart.

"Not all clear," the unfamiliar individual said in a cool and calm voice, and then laughed, "*Hyeh, hyeh, hyeh . . .*"

Rob stared, the hair rising on the back of his neck. "*You're* Termite?"

"In the flesh." The woman who held Frida at sword-point appeared absolutely ordinary. Her short, dark hair matched her dark eyes, which were framed by squarish, plastic-rimmed glasses that sat on her freckled nose. Her nose was neither large nor small. But something about the set of her lips gave away her true character. These were lips that could scold a crying child, insult a little old lady, or order an execution with equal relish.

"But . . . you're not supposed to be . . ."

"Here?" she put in mildly. "In my own room?" Evil filled her blackish-brown eyes. "I think it's you who are not supposed to be here." She advanced another step, and Frida tripped over the pile of sticks.

Rob sprang forward to help her up, but the griefer homed her blade in on Frida and said, "Not so fast, Roberto."

How does she know my real name? For some reason, that thought scared him more than anything else he'd heard from her so far.

"Let her go!" Rob said.

Again came that horrible laugh from the type of harmless-looking woman he would've punched a door open for if he'd met her in town.

Termite shook her head slowly. "If only you would have done as I asked."

Frida and Turner glanced at the captain, wondering what he hadn't told them.

"Selling out the Overworld isn't something I *could* do," Rob retorted. "I'm just one guy. The United Biomes act together."

"Kind of like you and Lady Craven," Turner said evenly to Termite. "Pals, ain't ya?"

"She's your boss, isn't she?" Frida needled the griefer.

Termite remained unruffled. "Boss. Employee. The distinction eludes me."

"So, you do what you do because you *like* doin' it?" Turner said disparagingly.

"Like, dislike. Just words. Kind of like *life* and *death*." Her lips compressed in a parody of a smile. She poked her sword at Frida. "I understand how running with this battalion can make you feel . . . claustrophobic. Groups are tricky things. For instance, a unified Overworld? Example of a bad group. Unified hostile mobs? Now that group suits me just fine."

Unifying the zombies and skeletons through enchantment was how the Griefer Imperial Army had divided the biomes. Rob's battalion had repeatedly fought back, first against Dr. Dirt, and later, against his successor, Lady Craven. As Jools had observed, she was probably responsible for the eastern mob export that Gaia had warned them of.

"So, if you're working on your own, why do you care about the GIA or the UBO?" Rob asked.

She gave another dry, lifeless chuckle. "My relationship with Lady Craven goes as far as her powers can help me. Of course, she thinks it's the other way around. And now, I must go meet my legions of undead worshippers at the minecart station. Will you be so kind as to empty your inventories?"

The troopers knew a mandatory request when they heard one. Their sundry food, weapons, ammo, armor, and crafting ingredients were swiftly moved from their possession to Termite's. Then she calmly and deliberately sheathed her sword, and made for the door.

"I'm sorry you'll miss the fireworks," she said in a voice so utterly full of condescension that Rob thought he'd be sick. Termite stepped into the dark corridor. "Oh, and don't open the door." She paused. "It's booby-trapped."

*

Now the troopers knew where the bomb materials had gone—to rig the chamber as a death trap. Being free to move about but stuck in the small bunker gave Rob a feeling not unlike his fall from thirty thousand feet. He'd had time to admire the view on the way down, but those last few blocks were doozies.

With no other ideas, Frida and Turner waited for their commanding officer to take charge.

"What do you think, sir?" she finally asked him.

Turner raised his eyebrows. "Well?"

Rob opened his mouth, and then closed it again. The evil griefer was loose, hordes of zombies were on their way into town, and the celebrating villagers would have no warning whatsoever. Despite that ugly equation, all Rob could think about was that he hadn't yet slept in a bed. "What's going to happen to us?" he said out loud.

Frida was still hopeful. "The others'll notice we're missing and come looking."

Turner snorted. "After they fight off an army of hostiles on their own? I doubt it. Naw, it's up to us to find a way out." He marched over to the dungeon. "Could be somethin' useful in here that I can whack stuff with."

"I wouldn't whack too hard," Frida advised. "We don't know what the trigger perimeter is."

Turner crept back toward her and Rob, his face shiny with sweat. "Then I'ma whack *him*." He feigned a punch, and Rob instinctively put up a hand to block it. "You got us into this mess. Great plan, Newbie. Guess the bomb is on the other foot now."

Frida glanced at him. "What's that supposed to mean?"

Turner grunted. "Just, he's the one wanted us all to change our spawn points in case o' death, and now he's gonna get a taste of that. Ain't no tellin' where you'll end up," he said, his eyes drilling into Rob's.

As she watched the two, the truth dawned on Frida. She turned a hurt face toward Rob. "You mean, you never changed your spawn point?" He didn't answer. Anger crept into her voice. "And you planned for *us* to be the ones carrying the flag, if something happened to you?"

Her words pelted the captain like buckshot, careening off the walls in echoes of shame.

"I just . . . wanted to be able to go home, someday."

Frida's voice held a note of pleading. "And I wanted this to *be* your home."

Rob couldn't meet her gaze. The chances of getting out of this chamber alive were small. The odds of Rob respawning elsewhere were huge. And now, with the battalion split up and the others in grave danger, his failure to stand by his troops was complete.

*

The minutes ticked away. Somewhere above ground, a train of undead predators was unloading on a hundred men, women, and children who had only been looking for a better life. Belowground, three troopers were gradually coming to terms with their shortened futures.

This made Rob focus on his past. "If I was back home right now, we'd be moving the herd up to summer pasture," he said out loud, not caring if anyone was listening. "Pistol would be shedding like crazy. And Jip's coat'd be so full, I'd have to shear him like a sheep. . . ."

The likelihood that these were their final moments caused Frida and Turner to soften toward the captain—enough to speak to him, anyway.

"Then what would you do?" Frida asked.

The three sat in a row, cross-legged, against a wall. Rob stirred. "Well, now. There'd still be snow in the mountains. A few of the cows would've dropped calves, and the little ones can have a hard time crossing snowfields. We'd have our work cut out for us, bringing them up to the highlands safe and sound." He peeked at Frida and found he held her attention. "Heck, sometimes we'd lose a mama. Many's the time I've carried an orphan calf like a sack of potatoes over Pistol's withers. . . ."

Turner spoke up, less gruffly than usual. "You really b'lieve that? Think it's a real memory?"

Rob caught his eye. "I know it is. Don't you have 'em?"

The mercenary hesitated. "I do. Ain't as purty as yours, but I do."

"You never told me that, Meat. Like what?" Frida asked.

Turner thought. "There was times, after a big storm, when I'd go huntin'." He thought some more. "Monster hurricane'd let loose folkses' pets."

"Ugh." Rob drew back. "You'd shoot people's pets?"

"Not Fluffy and Fifi, mind you," Turner said hastily. "No, there was folks'd put a python in a fish tank and let it grow. Thought it was cute till it got outdoors, started breedin' in the swamp."

"You shot people's *snakes*?" Rob said.

Turner nodded. "Once the local authorities dried out their basements, they'd put a bounty on them giants. So's they wouldn't eat people's kids."

"What's a—snake?" Frida asked.

Rob regarded her. "You mean, you don't remember?"

"I don't know."

Rob shot Turner a questioning look.

"Some players been in this game so long, they don't remember their old life," he explained.

Frida frowned. "That's not it. I come from the jungle."

Rob touched her arm. "Maybe another jungle. We have them in my world, too. That's where snakes live."

Turner shifted on the floor. "Bayou's a lot like a jungle," he said.

"No," Frida protested. "This jungle. I'm sure of it."

Just then, they heard noise outside the bunker. The door slid open, and a body was dumped at their feet.

CHAPTER 16

THE TROOPERS SAW TERMITE'S FACE EMERGE FROM the shadows. "Now, this one will pay for your little trick!"

To Rob's relief—and dread—she didn't wait around for a reply.

The door slid shut and they heard a menacing *click*. But Rob thought the griefer's voice had sounded slightly strained.

"Jools! What happened?"

The quartermaster groaned and lifted his head. "Captain! What are you chaps doing in here?" He joined them in their row against the wall.

They gave him a summary of their silverfish melee and retreat, and subsequent capture. He told them that Turner's minecart scheme had worked—to an extent.

"My Thunder Boys were able to place round-house tracks just south of the city, leaving the old ones as dummies. Termite had no idea the incoming carts would be shunted right back the way they came. What we failed to anticipate was that she'd still make her original rendezvous point . . . and that I'd be there, twiddling my thumbs. More's the pity. The control tower would've been an excellent seat for the fireworks."

"And the Thunder Boys?" Rob asked.

"After their hard work, I gave them the night off. They were last seen nibbling on candy floss and elephant ears."

"But, what about the others?" asked Frida, fearing the worst.

"None the wiser," Jools said. "Kim was in the center ring with her horses, and Stormie was prepping the whizz-bangs when Termite got to me. The judge and colonel had been playing those dreary games of chance with the settlers, but they seemed to be enjoying themselves."

This illustration of the carefree scene caused fear to knife through Rob's gut. Not only had he put dozens of innocent people in harm's way, his mentor—the colonel—and his friend—the judge—might meet the fates they had dodged so many times before.

"What do you think Termite's intentions are?" Rob asked Jools.

"Impossible to calculate. She's . . . unpredictable, to say the least." He got to his feet and started checking out the confines. "So, how about getting out of here?"

No one said anything.

"We . . . *are* getting out of here," he said less decisively.

"The door's rigged with a bomb," Frida explained.

"I reckon old Termite'll keep us in here till the ribbon cuttin'," Turner added. "Then blow the thing."

"I see," said Jools.

"You might want to get your affairs in order," Rob suggested.

Jools gave a weak laugh. "And to whom would I leave my things? You are all right here."

The implication sent a faint warmth through the cavalry commander's icy body. "You must have someone else you care about. You know, we were just talking about our other lives," Rob said. "In the other world. Before the game started."

"What? That? Oh, my. That's ancient history."

"Yeah, but it's something no one can take away," Rob asserted. "You must have a past. A . . . mother. We all do."

Jools deflected the comment, tilting his head at Turner. "You're not saying *he's* got a mum."

Turner sat up straighter. "Who'd ya think give me these good looks?"

Frida leaned across Rob. "Come on, Jools. We all came into this world. My beginnings were with—Apple Corps." Her voice broke as she used the nickname for her family clan. "I expected my end would be there, too."

"Well, I'm not going back," Jools remarked with bitterness. "That's why I switched my spawn point like Rob asked. Even if I die a thousand deaths, I'll not rejoin that lot of unfeeling wretches. Dad was a tax man. He was never home. Mum only had eyes for my little brother."

"But . . . didn't you have friends?" Frida asked timidly.

"It's them that were the worst! There I was, off for an afternoon of multiplayer gaming with the lads. It'd be fun, they promised. We'd be a cracking team. Next I knew, they hung me out to dry like a fortnight's worth of dirty laundry."

Jools described one mate as obsessed with amassing gems, the other with increasing XP—and neither of them having his back when it came time to fight off hostile mobs.

"Did you . . . die?" asked Rob.

"Did I ever. Over and over, like the world would never end. I didn't know it at the time, but my so-called mates used some fancy cheats to avoid death. Every time I croaked and came back, it was me setting out to find them. When I finally did, they'd fix on some personal agenda, only to let *me* get snuffed when *I* held off the zombies for *them*." He failed to keep the note of bitterness out of his voice.

Turner scoffed, "Sounds like men who ain't got no code."

"Not a shred of decency," Jools confirmed. "Eventually, I vowed to ally myself with no one, rather than be sold out again."

Rob and the others were shocked to hear these intimate details from the normally stoic quartermaster. "So . . . that's why you became a contract worker," Rob concluded.

"A freelancer, yes. Detail management was already in my blood. I acted as a consultant to any organization that would pay me, before I met up with you."

"Them as can pay generally don't give a rat's behind whether ya live or die," Turner reflected.

"But at least they're honest about it," Jools said.

Rob tried to make him feel better. "You've done well for yourself in the Overworld, though. Put your skills to good use. We couldn't have made it this far without your genius for strategy."

"If only I had been more on point this time around," Jools said sadly. "I will miss Mum's mince-meat," he admitted. "And little Ian's somewhat exasperating behavior."

"Ian? Is that your brother?" Frida asked.

"Yes. He's a good lad. I'll miss him."

Now Turner's voice rose by a half-octave. "You ain't givin' up, are ya? What about all that genius-brain stuff? So my plot coulda been . . . tighter. Why don't you give it another whirl, Sir Thinks-a-lot?"

Jools put his hands on his hips. "You're telling *me* to bail us out? It was your daft idea that put us here."

"Troops," Rob said tiredly, "I don't think arguing will open that door any faster."

They heard a scuffle outside, and a shout. Then the barrier between the troopers and freedom slid open again. This time, Stormie and Kim, trussed with spider string, were pushed into the chamber. They fell heavily in a heap. The door swung shut, and they heard footsteps on stone retreating down the tunnel.

Frida and Turner unwrapped their captive friends. Kim and Stormie rubbed their wrists, took a few steps, and then slumped to the floor.

"We put up a fight, Captain," Kim said wearily.

"But the griefer had help," Stormie put in. "Could've been that Volt character."

Everyone's health had suffered, and their inventories had been emptied. Now, the entire battalion was weak, trapped, and weaponless. Their situation had never been this dire.

"I hope the colonel and the judge are all right," Stormie worried. "Maybe they can get us out of here."

"They're probably next on Termite's list," Jools predicted.

Kim moaned. "Who'll take care of the horses?" She dropped her head and buried it in her arms.

This jolted Rob out of his melancholy. As usual, the selfless horse master had put the animals' welfare before her own. He owed it to her to ease her pain, if he could.

Colonel M had taught him that company morale was a double-edged sword that could be used for or against him. Rob had to keep spirits up and make sure that if anybody was going to die, it wouldn't be by their own hands. "Say, Corporal," he said gently to Kim. "We were just talking about old times. Before the game. Why don't you tell us how you got into horses?"

She didn't respond.

"Come on, bronc whisperer," Stormie urged. "We'd like to hear about it."

*

A true horse master can't resist talking about her equine friends. After some more encouragement, the group persuaded Kim to tell her story.

"We lived up north," she said. "My family trained the national breed of horses, but I was just a little thing." She realized that she still was, and gave a tiny, hollow laugh. "I wasn't big enough to ride yet, and I wanted a puppy dog for my very own."

Jools appeared touched. He murmured, "So did I, once."

Kim dove further into her tale. "Well, Appa and Omma—that's what I called my dad and mum—they wouldn't let me have a dog. They said I wouldn't be able to take care of it."

"Why not?" Frida asked.

"Don't know. I decided I'd show them." Kim gave a small smile. "I ran away from home—I knew where there was a pet shop. I went in and picked out the puppy I wanted, and the nice owner said he'd send it home with me. He went and called my folks."

Rob interrupted. "I don't see how this got you into horses."

"Shh!" Turner waved an arm and leaned forward. "Then what happened?"

"While I was waiting for Appa and Omma to pick me up, the pet shop man let me play games on his computer. I got lost, and killed, and respawned—in the middle of a horse pasture," Kim explained.

"And what—you're saying wild horses raised you?" Jools joked.

She nodded seriously. "They did. This one stallion—I named him Jim—he was smarter than most people. He taught me everything I needed to know."

"And you'd lived out in horse country ever since? Until you found us?"

She nodded. Satisfied, she sat back against the wall.

"I can't imagine staying in one place like that," Stormie mused.

"But *you* must have started out somewhere," Rob prompted.

"I was an army brat. We moved all over. Guess you could say I had six or eight homes—or none, really."

Turner cocked his head. "So, becomin' a professional tramp weren't much of a stretch then."

She gave a wry smile. "If you want to put it that way, yeah. Once I hit the game, I started walking and just kept going. Turned out I could make gems by sellin' information I picked up along the way—locations for the best farming, ore deposits, view properties . . ."

"And you could steer people off of witch swamps, et cetera," Jools said.

Stormie nodded. "I'da kept goin' forever, but then I ran into Lady Craven, and then I ran into y'all . . . So, here I am."

These words brought them back to reality.

"Here we all are," Rob echoed.

"Well, not all of us . . ." Stormie pointed out.

As if to emphasize this, the door slid open yet again. But this time, no one but Termite entered.

The griefer tossed two items into the chamber. Rob collected them, recognizing them immediately: one was Judge Tome's old UBO ring, and the other was a crumpled print-out of Colonel M's ribbon-cutting speech.

"Those belong to the judge and the colonel." Rob felt terror rise in his chest. "I'll kill you, you scum!" He leapt up and threw himself at Termite.

The composed criminal calmly drew a golden axe and knocked him down with its handle. A thin trickle of blood ran from the corner of his mouth.

Frida jumped to his aid but drew back when Termite threatened her with the gleaming blade. "Thanks for all the gold, by the way," the griefer said in her measured speech. "Your villagers won't be needing it."

"Wh-what have you done with them?" Frida ventured.

"Not a thing. They will make their own decisions to vacate this wasteland when the time comes."

Stormie retorted, "They'll build it up again. Even if you bomb the city, you'll never weaken folkses' taste for freedom."

"Hyeh, hyeh, hyeh . . ." The humorless laugh made Rob cringe. Termite gazed down on Stormie as though she were a bug. "I couldn't care less about your city. Nor could those little people. It's you six they look up to. And with you gone . . . I'll wager they won't be quite so hungry for freedom anymore."

Kim narrowed her eyes. "You meant to capture us all along? Why didn't you do it before? You had any number of chances."

Termite's lips twitched. "And miss this drama? Perish the thought." She jerked her head back. "No, perish you! You and your silly captain." She retreated to the door. "You were such easy marks. The name 'Battalion Zero' really suits you."

This backhanded compliment put a damper on what little courage the troopers had left. But Rob rallied his. "And the name 'Termite' suits you!"

The slur enraged the unstable griefer. "Your anguish will know no bounds, cowboy! You have yet to experience the highlight of my final act for you." She backed into the corridor's gloom. Before sealing them in, she shrieked, "This bomb? The trigger has a five-second delay."

*

Rob's mind spun. How was a long fuse a greater threat than they already faced? As Kim, Frida, and Stormie converged in a frightened hug, the captain turned to the sergeant and quartermaster. "What does that mean?"

With the burden of understanding, Jools said, "That means that someone can escape . . . and the rest of us will die."

"And probably be buried under the rubble," Turner added.

Rob's heart thudded to earth. He wouldn't abandon his friends again. "I could never live with that."

"Me, neither," Frida said.

Jools shook his head sadly. "I always thought there'd be . . . another tomorrow." He choked on the last words.

Turner growled, "Nobody's tomorrow is guaranteed." But the mercenary wasn't through yet. "We could make some noise," he offered. "Start yellin'— some guard is bound to hear us."

Tears sprang to Stormie's eyes. "And just wait until some poor, innocent villager tries to rescue us and gets blown to smithereens? I don't think so."

Kim looked around helplessly. "So, I guess we're stuck here, then."

Nobody replied.

Slowly, the light returned to Jools's expression. ". . .maybe not." His words hung in the air.

Rob raised his head. "I'm listening."

Jools repeated that the trigger delay would allow someone to make it out the open door before the bomb went off. "Five seconds . . . I'm thinking, two of us could get out of here. Might not make it in one piece, but there's a chance."

Stormie wiped away her tears and thought this over. "Could work. Two of us could escape and try to salvage what's left of the city—maybe get a piece of Termite before she gets away. Frida, Turner, seein' as how y'all never changed spawn points, I reckon you'd be the logical choices to go."

Rob's face went red. The two survivalists glanced at each other, and then at the captain.

He cleared his throat. "Uh, the truth is, I didn't change my spawn point, either."

This floored the others.

"But Stormie's right." He eyed Frida and Turner. "You two should go. Get away. Maybe the rest'll respawn in camp." Rob couldn't even begin to fathom where he might wind up.

It was the sergeant's turn to look uncomfortable. "Fact is, Captain, I did follow orders," he mumbled. "Just last night."

Now everyone's face showed disbelief.

Jools found his voice first. "*You* changed your spawn point? You—the mighty mercenary, master of your own fortune. . . . You're telling me *you* knuckled under and threw in with the group?" He seemed to have forgotten that fighting with Turner might not pay off. In a passable imitation, he lowered his voice and said, "*Harrumph.* Man's spawn point oughta be kept secret. What's the Overworld comin' to?" He failed to get a rise out of Turner.

The subdued mercenary explained, "Was Rose did it to me. After she turned sour, I figured I could still come out ahead if I respawned along with the folks who really matter. So I switched spawn points."

Rob's mouth fell open. Hearing this almost made up for facing an untimely death.

"Naw," Turner went on, "it's you two should go, Cap'n." He turned to Frida. "Unless . . . *you* got somethin' you ain't tellin' us."

Frida's skin deepened by a shade of green. "Uh, sorry, Meat. Nope."

Rather than being disappointed in her, Rob felt a surge of a much deeper emotion. Frida was a creature of the jungle—of the Overworld jungle, if she was right about her origins. If she died and came back into the game, there was no place else for her to call home.

Rob reached out and took her hand, and squeezed it hard. "Come on," he said, his voice barely above a whisper.

Frida addressed the group. "Are you all . . . sure?"

They gave her their silent blessing.

Frida hung back a moment. Then she scrambled to her feet and said to the others, "Take cover. We—we'll see you back in camp."

The troopers nodded.

Rob switched on his headlamp, pressed on the door, and—without looking back—pulled Frida through it after him.

*

The blast was louder than anything Rob had ever heard. He felt the concussion slam through his chest and shoot him down the tunnel.

"Frida!" he screamed.

For a moment, nothing but the sound of tumbling rock and rumbling earth filled his injured ears. Then, miraculously, she answered.

Half-blind and half-deaf, Rob crawled toward the faint sound of her voice and felt for her. "It's gonna come down. Run!" Again he grabbed her hand and pulled them both up, moving like there was no tomorrow. The weight of leaving his troops behind could not stop his heart and mind from propelling him forward, upward, and into the light with Frida.

They ran. They kept running until they reached the city garden, far enough to escape the debris that rained down from the cliffside. Then they turned and watched where the opening had been. They waited, hoping, as block upon block of falling stone made it clear that no living being would emerge from the wreckage.

After moments or hours—Rob wasn't sure which— he tugged at Frida's hand, and against her objections, pulled her down the main street, through the gaping chainmail fence, and back toward cavalry camp.

Movement in the distance caught Rob's eye. It looked as though there was life down there yet. Whatever they'd left behind, they owed it to the people to move forward, to go through with their mission.

Frida stopped and looked over her shoulder. "D'you think they'll make it?" she asked, meaning Kim, Jools, Stormie, and Turner.

"If they didn't take too much damage." Rob pulled Frida to him and hung on for a moment, before letting her go. "With any luck, we'll all be right back where we started this morning." He paused. "Right?"

Frida didn't answer.

"At least it's something," he said.

She pushed away a tear. "Not much."

But Rob could see she didn't mean it. Maybe she felt as bad as he did about not changing spawn points. Anyone could tell they were both committed to the battalion, heart and soul. After all they'd been through, they still believed in the Overworld, still believed in their friends—and in each other.

"Hey." He looked Frida in the eye and said truthfully, "Might not be much. But it's enough."

CHECK OUT THE REST OF THE DEFENDERS OF THE OVERWORLD SERIES

AND JOIN BATTALION ZERO'S QUEST:

The Battle of Zombie Hill

NANCY OSA

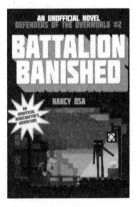

Battalion Banished

NANCY OSA

Deep Ocean Six

NANCY OSA

DO YOU LIKE FICTION FOR MINECRAFTERS?

Check out other unofficial Minecrafter adventures from Sky Pony Press!

Invasion of the Overworld
MARK CHEVERTON

Battle for the Nether
MARK CHEVERTON

Confronting the Dragon
MARK CHEVERTON

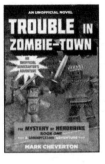

Trouble in Zombie-town
MARK CHEVERTON

The Quest for the Diamond Sword
WINTER MORGAN

The Mystery of the Griefer's Mark
WINTER MORGAN

The Endermen Invasion
WINTER MORGAN

Treasure Hunters in Trouble
WINTER MORGAN

Available wherever books are sold!

LIKE OUR BOOKS
FOR MINECRAFTERS?

Then check out other novels
by Sky Pony Press.

Pack of Dorks
BETH VRABEL

**Boys Camp:
Zack's Story**
CAMERON DOKEY,
CRAIG ORBACK

**Boys Camp:
Nate's Story**
KITSON JAZYNKA,
CRAIG ORBACK

**Letters from an
Alien Schoolboy**
R. L. ASQUITH

**Just a Drop of
Water**
KERRY O'MALLEY
CERRA

Future Flash
KITA HELMETAG
MURDOCK

Sky Run
ALEX SHEARER

Mr. Big
CAROL AND MATT
DEMBICKI

Available wherever books are sold!